I0594374

# Dark World

**An Echo's Way Adventure**

by

## Mike Waller

# Books by Mike Waller

## The 'ECHO'S WAY Series

Solitude's End – An Echo's Way Adventure
Dark World – An Echo's Way Adventure
Enemy Ally – An Echo's Way Adventure

## The FALCON Trilogy

Falcon's Call
Falcon's Ghost
Falcon's Bane

## Other

Hawk: Hellfire
Brothers Of Mind

Published by Rampart Publishing

ISBN 9780648275503

Cover by 100 covers

This is a work of fiction. All characters are fictional, and bare no relation to any person or persons living or dead.

# The 'ECHO'S WAY' Adventures

The Echo's Way stories relate the adventures of Echo Bourke, a remarkable young woman who finds herself embroiled against her will in the harsh reality of a war between the Federation of Humanity and a powerful alien neighbor, the Tolleani.

Each Book is a separate adventure, rather than part of a continuing, single story. There are no 'to be continued's and no cliff-hanger endings. Each book can be read as a stand-alone story in the life of our heroine.

**Dark World** is the second adventure in Echo Bourke's journey, and tells of how she survives a pirate attack when on her way to join the military academy, then helps the locals on a lost planet rise up against the pirate family who have oppressed them.

This book utilizes US English spelling.

# *Contents*

# Chapter One

BEN LET HIS MIND wander as images of Echo drifted through his consciousness. A vague smile flickered across his lips as he pictured her angelic face. Why she stayed with him was beyond comprehension, but she did, and Ben counted his blessings.

He remembered how she ran her fingers across the ever-present stubble on his chin and along the line of strange characters tattooed down his right flank. He knew those characters fascinated her, but in all the time he had known her, their meaning had remained a secret. She believed they held a great secret, perhaps a love or tragedy from a past time, and he did not want to disillusion her with the knowledge that they were meaningless.

He remembered also the place where they first laid eyes on each other. *Corros! The prospector's cabin, that's where.* High in the forested mountains of Echo's home world, the old cabin was warm and welcoming. *We destroyed that place. The forest, the mine, the town ... gone ... forever!*

An urgent, buzzing sound sounded at the edge of his consciousness. The alarm wormed its way into his brain, the irritation growing louder and more persistent with each passing second. Eyes half open, he continued to stare up at the dull, gray ceiling in the master's cabin of his new ship.

After escaping from the now Tolleani-controlled planet, he and Echo were at first never apart. With his resumption of duty and reassignment, it had been over a month since they had last been together.

Their escape was a year ago. Prior to that, Echo spent four years alone, the sole survivor of an invasion that killed every other colonist in the planet's three mining settlements.

Sent to investigate the chance of re-taking the colony, Ben's spacecraft crash-landed when attacked by an unknown prototype weapon at an alien research base occupying one of the mine sites. Not long after capture, he escaped from the Tolleani and stumbled upon Echo's refuge in the forested canyons of the surrounding mountains. Only with her help did he survive. Twice, she saved his life.

Now they were together. The knowledge that she would wait for him until this mission ended did little to ease the pain of separation by light years of space.

Irritated by the interruption, he dragged himself to the edge of the bunk, yawned, and scratched at the stubble on his chin. A slap on the intercom screen stopped the annoying buzz.

"Yes, Jerry?"

"Sorry to disturb you, Cap," a voice replied. "A distress call just came in on the common band. Thought you ought to know."

Ben pushed up from the berth and tumbled into the opposite bulkhead. The mission was several weeks old now, but after months either in hibernation or planet-bound, returning to the routine of life in a zero-gravity tin-can required a certain re-adjustment. Every lapse of attention resulted in a new bruise.

\*   \*   \*

Jerry Bayer, the first officer, was the only other person on the control deck. With a quick nod of acknowledgement Ben turned to the command console.

"Status?"

"The gateway to the *Arpeche* System's ahead, Captain. We're twenty hours from the jump point, and the ship sending the signal is sitting in front of the gate."

Ben floated into the captain's chair and studied the screens. "Hmm … fine. Keep monitoring it, and keep your wits about you. We've had a few unexplained disappearances in this sector recently, so keep your eyes open."

This ship was his first command, granted soon after promotion to captain. Most of the credit belonged to Echo; without her, he would have died long ago, somewhere in the wasteland now covering the site of her childhood home.

Six months after their return to *Cymbel 3* he received his bars and orders—with the war in full swing and humanity losing, the commission was inevitable—and with them came the command of a brand new destroyer.

Even now, a modified version of the Tollean device used to bring his last vessel down was being installed on Fleet's front line ships. No reports were in yet on the weapon's effectiveness. With the first fitted little more than a month ago, that did not surprise Ben: word was slow to travel in space. This destroyer carried one of the units, still untested in action.

*Give it time*, he thought. *The research Echo and I stole will bring an end to this war … or at least a compromise.*

Jerry interrupted his thoughts. "Captain, the signal isn't from a Fleet vessel, but it's certainly a distress call. Someone's in trouble."

"What do we know?"

"There's a Terran vessel, a '*CS34*' class, sitting in front of the gateway. Human, not Tollean. The request is on the general band, but no security codes."

"Civilian? Okay, send an acknowledgement. Get me a visual as soon as you can."

The image on the monitor was a short-haul freighter, old and worn but with no visible damage. It drifted in the middle of a region of empty space otherwise referred to as a gateway, containing the entrance to the *Arpeche 497* wormhole. On the side of the hull, faded and flaked paint spelled out the number '*10739*'.

"The computer has no record of that registration, Captain," Jerry said. "Must be from an unaligned planet." Dozens of worlds throughout the occupied galaxy had either left the Federation of Humanity or never joined. Many of them had fallen to the Tolleani, unnoticed beneath the radar.

Ben donned his headset. "Freighter 10739, this is Terran fleet destroyer G4973, Ben Teague commanding. Please advise your situation."

Several minutes later, a soft, feminine voice responded. "Captain Teague, Julia Ellis here. You cannot imagine how happy I am you're here. Thank you for responding."

"My pleasure, Captain Ellis. Again, what is your status?"

"My engines are down. An explosion in the engineering module occurred as we exited the gate from *Arpeche*. The damage is repairable, but my engineer is injured. I would appreciate your help and medical attention for my crewman."

Ben acknowledged without a moment's hesitation. Not responding to a distress call in space was contrary to regulation and had severe consequences. "My engineering officer will cross with our paramedic as soon as we rendezvous."

"Would linking our ships be possible?" Ellis asked. "My casualty is in a critical condition, and we have no facilities. His leg is broken, so we can't get him into a suit. I have a transfer pod, but I need your inter-lock tube to bring him across to you."

"Sorry, no. You're not broadcasting an approved security code. Fleet regulations do not permit a link with any vessel unless it correctly identifies itself."

"My apologies, Captain. This ship is an unaligned freelance surveyor and not part of the Federation. We've not been home for three months and don't have your codes, so we can't verify ourselves. Perhaps your people can check us over, and then you might agree to a connection?"

For a moment, Ben pondered the situation. To give help in a medical emergency was obligatory under Fleet regulations, but he would not put his command at risk. "I'll let you know when we come alongside. Stand by."

Hours later, the old freighter drifted beside them in space, less than a hull's length separating the two ships.

"Looks harmless enough," Jerry said. "Doesn't appear to be any visible damage. I have six heat signatures inside, one prone."

"Send Raj and Miko across, and we'll wait for their report."

Thirty minutes later, the voice of Ben's medical officer, Miko, came over the speaker. "Captain, everything appears in order here. The patient's femur is broken; he has serious blood loss and is unconscious. We need to set up the tunnel to bring him over so I can stabilize him and repair the leg. This ship has no facilities."

Ben noticed more than usual stress in Miko's voice. "You *are* aware, Fleet regulations do not allow me to approve a direct connection until I am satisfied there is no threat?" he said.

"Yes sir. The regulations also require us to help wherever possible when lives are at risk. This man will die unless he gets attention." Miko's voice was forced and showed obvious concern.

"Can you do it there?"

"No. I can fix the fracture, but he needs transfusions. I need my medical bay. Benjamin, please. Regulation 973 requires me to help this man."

Once again, Ben could hear the tension in her voice. "Have you checked the ship?"

"Yes, everything is ten-ten. Raj is heading back to the engine module now. Benjamin, it's just what you would expect of a surveyor."

Ben looked across to his second in command. "Miko's upset about something, wouldn't you say?"

"Distraught, I guess. Doesn't surprise me. The worst she gets on this boat is a vitamin deficiency and headaches; now she has a potentially critical condition. She called you Benjamin."

"She's never addressed me by my name before, much less 'Benjamin'—always *Captain*. And ten-ten? Have you ever heard of regulation 973?"

Jerry shook his head. "Can't find it on the computer. She's trying to tell us something."

A direct connection with an unknown ship was contrary to orders and an enormous risk, and Miko's words indicated there was a problem she could not talk about. If anything happened, the result would be a loss of command for Ben. There was, according to his medical officer, a life in danger, and other regulations dictated that help must be provided. The vessel was Terran—that at least, was clear. Ben considered the options. *Dammed if I do...*

"Alright," he said, "we'll set up now, Miko." The risk, he decided, was unavoidable. "Captain Ellis will cross with you, plus the patient and Raj. Nobody else. As soon as you're aboard, I'll meet with her. You will all remain in the bay, and I'll come to you."

"Yes, Sir."

Ben switched to the internal intercom. "Bayliss, you and Mahib get down to the airlock. Set up the link tunnel as quickly as possible, carry your side arms, and be wary. The visitors are not permitted to leave the bay under any circumstances. You will keep them under guard until I get there."

Flicking the intercom off, he turned to Jerry. "We need to get our people out of there. I have serious concerns about this."

Something troubled him about the whole situation. The prospector showed no obvious sign of external damage, but Ellis had explained there was an isolated explosion inside the engine room. The scanners confirmed the engines were cold.

Uncomfortable with the docking tube, he was even more so with leaving a civilian spacecraft helpless and an unconscious, injured man without hope. Miko's speech also concerned him; clearly, she had attempted to tell him something under duress.

*She's never addressed me by my name before.*

"On their way now," Jerry said. "Four persons crossing: Miko with the patient in a stretcher, Raj assisting, and Captain Ellis."

Ben watched on the intercom as the arrivals approached the airlock and moved into the bay. He rose and glided back towards his cabin, thinking it a coincidence the disabled ship should malfunction right on the entrance to the wormhole, the one place in the vastness of space with a guarantee of early rescue. Again, Ellis had an explanation that they had just exited the gateway.

He retrieved his sidearm; armed, with the crew in the docking bay, he was at least prepared if anything went wrong. Returning to the bridge, he was about to head back to the bay when the hatch to the control deck burst open.

A middle-aged male wearing Raj's pressure suit floated through, a laser pistol in his hand. Behind him, a woman, also armed and threatening, and wearing Miko's pressure suit, pulled herself through the opening.

The man holding the gun was tall and rangy with blonde, thinning hair and a stubbled chin. Green eyes glittered in the cockpit lights as he glanced around, an almost euphoric look on his face. Focusing his attention on Ben, he licked his lips as if savoring a tasty dish or a fine wine. "Please stay in your seat, Captain," he said, "and keep your hands away from the console."

"Who in the Hells are you? Where is my crew?"

"Your engineer and paramedic are safe on board my ship. My worthy associates are attending to your men in the bay. Oh, and your vessel is now my property."

The woman, most likely the same who identified herself as Captain Ellis, smiled as her companion spoke. The man peered around the cabin again, a broad Cheshire-cat grin spread across his face.

"A Fleet destroyer," he crowed. "I am going to find this *so* useful."

# Chapter Two

FIELD-GENERAL BRADFORD MILLINER dropped the application on the desk and peered through aged, watery, brown eyes at the young woman seated opposite. "So you hope to enter the academy, my dear?"

"Yes, Sir."

Cinta 'Echo' Bourke sat bolt upright, looking increasingly unsure with each passing moment. Next to Ben, the general had been her strongest supporter; he would do anything to help her, but this request was a long stretch.

She had made her application despite a single good reason for Fleet accepting her. At twenty-three years of age she was too old for normal traineeship admission and had no educational qualifications working in her favor. Molliner thought her decision had most likely been spontaneous, born from sheer frustration, boredom, and the need for a new purpose.

The battered, old stalwart peered over his spectacles. The girl was young, vibrant, and attractive, with long, brown hair. Her deep-green, almond-shaped eyes could bore into a man, leaving him lost and wondering what he was missing.

Molliner felt he could rise above the emotion. At seventy-one, he understood well the feelings he held for Echo. There was love there, he knew, but love as a father for a daughter. That was how he felt about this amazing young woman.

*But one is never too old to appreciate beauty,* he thought.

This woman differed from most he had met before. Cinta Bourke commanded his deepest respect from what she had been through in her life so far, and her activities in the recent past.

A little more than a year ago, she had escaped a Tolleani-occupied planet, and in the process rescued a Fleet naval officer and destroyed a Tollean weapons research base. She and Ben Teague secured priceless alien data and handed it over to the naval authorities on their arrival here.

Over time, Molliner came to consider her a daughter. She had nobody else, having lost her entire family in the attack on her home world. Teague became her life partner after their escape, but had been listed as missing in action several months ago.

"Do you think they will accept my application?" Echo asked, clearly expecting a negative response.

"Well... yes, I think so. Fleet owes you quite a debt. The data you brought from *Corros* could make all the difference in this war."

Echo's attention lifted a notch; a positive answer was unexpected. "Nothing has been said to me about that since I arrived here."

"No, I expect not. The whole thing is classified, and you're a civilian, so you've never heard what I'm about to tell you. Understand?"

Echo nodded as Molliner leaned forward, rested both elbows on his desk, and peered over the rim of his spectacles the way he did whenever he wished to talk of matters serious.

17

"Young lady, I'm an old man. The brass can't do much to me now and I'm close to retirement—would be now if not for this damned war. I'll tell you this because I think you should know, but you keep it to yourself. Agreed?"

Again, Echo nodded, sensing the General was about to tell her something she did not want to hear, but aware also that nothing she said would stop him.

"The device that disabled Ben's vessel is a remarkable achievement," he said. "It sends out an electronic signal that locks onto a target's computer systems, allows the attacking ship's computers to identify the various circuits on the enemy vessel, then singles out specific circuitry and shuts it down. The experts believe a targeted beam can be effective across hundreds of kilometers of space."

Molliner eased back from the desk. "The Tollean scientists may not have reported their results back to their superiors before you took them out, since there are no reports of their using it against us other than on *Corros*. That was a test run, I expect, and they intended further development before handing it over. We, however, are installing the first units in our front-line ships at this moment. This will change the war for us, thanks to you."

"Thanks to Ben!"

"Yes, Captain Teague, of course."

"What about the other thing? The super-bomb?"

"Ah, well, don't know if I should talk about that." For a moment, Molliner studied his visitor before continuing.

"All hush-hush at present, so you did not hear this from me either. Should anyone ever question you, say you saw it on your home world and overheard gossip somewhere. Dream something up, yes?"

Echo nodded, but remained silent.

"We think the theory was to create a trigger for a sustained atmospheric chain reaction, destroying every air-breathing organism on a planet. Lucky for you and Ben, the prototype was incomplete, and you didn't activate it in a proper manner—you would *not* be here otherwise. It seems unlikely, but our people tell us they might be able to complete the research. If successful, we will possess the deadliest weapon ever invented: a planet-buster that doesn't bust the planet."

Echo felt a heavy weight drop in her stomach. "That's monstrous. You're not suggesting we would use such a thing, even against the Tolleani?"

"Ah, but they intended to use it against us. Who knows if they are still working on the device, but we can't afford to ignore the possibility. If they complete it before we do, the human race will be extinct in a year. Don't forget who started this war."

For a moment, he sat back in his chair and peered at Echo. "Are you familiar with the atomic bomb attacks of Terran World War Two?"

"No. Should I be?"

"No, not at all, my dear, but let me enlighten you. Centuries ago, a great conflict occurred on the origin planet, *Old Earth*. Three nations, Germany, Italy, and Japan, joined forces to conquer the world, mainly for resources. The remaining nations allied to stop them.

"Towards the end of hostilities, both sides devoted massive resources to build the first working atom bomb, the forerunner of thermonuclear weapons. The Germans came close but were defeated before they could finish. Soon after, the United States, one of the defenders, succeeded, but by this time, only Japan was still fighting. The allied forces dropped an atomic device on the Japanese city of Hiroshima and a second on its near neighbor, Nagasaki. Japan surrendered within days. The death toll was appalling, but many experts believe the number of lives saved by the rapid ending of the conflict to be greater. To be fair, I should add the conclusion is debatable."

"So you're saying we should destroy a Tollean planet to end the war?"

"To bring the Tolleani to the negotiation table. It need not be an occupied world. We only want peace, not to conquer or kill. There is a great deal we could learn from them, and vice versa."

Echo sat staring at the floor, horrified that she had brought back such a weapon. Handing the stolen data block to the authorities had been a source of pride for her, but now she felt ashamed. Would history remember her as a hero or a monster?

*What will books say of me?* "You should not be telling me this."

"Of course not. It could be worth this old man's job, but I trust you to stay silent until the official announcements. With the bomb, that will be never, so keep it to yourself, please."

It was an order and not a request, Echo realized. She sighed, nodded agreement, and redirected her gaze back to her mentor. *Why tell me any of this?* "What does this have to do with joining Fleet?"

The General smiled at his visitor. "The service owes you a huge debt. Its gratitude will become official in three weeks, when you receive the Civil Cross."

Echo's mind snapped to attention at the mention of the well-known award. The *Cross* was the highest honor presented to non-military personnel for services in wartime, and was not often granted.

"You're joking, aren't you?"

"Not at all." A document containing a list of presentations for the annual awards ceremony slid across the desk towards Echo. Under the heading for civilian honors was a single name, *Cinta Bourke*. The news left her breathless and a little stunned.

Molliner placed yet another sheet of paper on the desk. "This is a directive regarding nominees to the academy. As a rule, Fleet only accepts candidates straight from school and with the best of results. The usual age for a candidate is seventeen or eighteen years."

"...and I am twenty-three, and all the records of my schooling were destroyed. The attack on *Corros* came the week before my final exams, so I never got to graduate."

"Quite. However, in the last twelve months, our losses have numbered over nine hundred ships and fourteen thousand personnel; a bad year for us. Fleet has directed all divisions to consider anybody who wants to volunteer, and facilities are in place to deal with applicants outside the norm. I intend to recommend your application based on your receiving the Civil Cross, your service to the war effort so far, and your experience with the Tolleani."

Echo sat in silence, lost for a response. This was beyond anything she expected, and she could only nod her head again. Since her arrival here, the old general had been a father in so many ways, and she owed him more than she could ever repay.

"The question is which career path you should pursue," he said. "Any ideas?"

"No, I've been too busy to think about it. I only want to do my part. I'll be happy as a ranker, anything."

Molliner stood and turned to gaze out over the space field that stretched for kilometers into the distance. At various points between the administration building and the horizon, spacecraft of different types and sizes landed or lifted off, going about the business of keeping the base supplied and safe. With the general shortage of personnel, it was child's play for anyone to get a berth these days, and Echo could easily walk into a 'grunt' position on any one of those ships.

"Not if I have any say in it," he muttered, turning back to the young woman. "You've done more for the empire than most, and you will not be a common grunt." Yet again, he pushed a file towards Echo.

"This is a complete report of the *Corros* affair by Lieutenant, now the late, Captain Benjamin Teague. Everything that happened is in here, including your contribution. Ben reports you showed courage, resourcefulness, and intelligence sufficient to make some of our front-line officers cringe with envy. A copy will accompany my report to Fleet recommending your admission to officer training. Coming from me, they *will* accept you!"

Echo shook her head to dispel the growing numbness. Never did she imagine she might be acceptable to the academy, much less for a commission. Words failed her as she stared blankly at Molliner.

"So," the General continued, "with the personal recommendation of the sector administrator, who happens to be a four-star field-general—that would be me—plus this report and your Civil Cross award, I suspect they will grab the chance to recruit you."

"But ... as an officer?"

"Why not? Things happen fast during wartime. Quite a number of our newer officers have bought their way in with position or wealth, and their abilities leave much to be desired. You have all the qualities we need. With your talent for mathematics, you will make an excellent navigator. From there, you can step up to second and first officer, and given time, a command of your own."

Molliner held up a hand in anticipation of Echo's objections. "Before you say anything, you're more than capable with the right training. You're an intelligent girl—not your fault your education was interrupted."

Again, lost for an adequate response, Echo nodded.

"Don't prove me wrong, my dear." The General reached into a drawer, removed a small cube, and placed it on the desk in front of her. "In normal times, we only take trainees fresh from school, so you won't be at much of a disadvantage other than from your provincial schooling, which was most likely lacking in certain areas.

"This data block contains training programs on mathematics, physics, astronomy, computer science, and so on. Your instructors will expect basic knowledge in these fields when you begin, so you should start now. You leave for the academy in four weeks, and you'll commence studies as soon as you arrive. For several weeks of the voyage, you'll be asleep, so don't waste time."

"No, Sir, of course not." Echo took the cube and slipped it into the pocket of her coat. "I don't know what to say. This is more than I expected."

"Much less than you deserve, my dear," Molliner said. "Now, you have three appointments to keep. A week from now, you'll receive the 'Cross' at the annual beat-up. The official notification will arrive in a few days. Wear a white dress-suit and put your hair up."

"Yes, sir."

"Second, you will present yourself for your higher education certificate examination." Molliner pushed another data block forward. "It's in two weeks, and it's five years since you did your schooling, so you need to brush up. The test material is on this, in the file titled 'examination'. It would be wise to refresh your memory a little."

Echo's heart skipped a beat. "Where do I go?"

"My secretary will give you the details on your way out."

"Yes, Sir. The third appointment?"

"My wife and I are expecting you for dinner tomorrow evening, in case you forgot. Carla is always complaining that she doesn't see you enough."

"Oh, yes." Echo breathed a sigh of relief.

"My life will be a misery when she learns I'm sending you to war. You are the daughter she never had, you know."

All of a sudden, the man across the desk was no longer the most powerful on the planet, having once again become the dear, old man who befriended her when Ben went missing in action. She owed General Molliner a great deal and did not intend to let him down.

\* \* \*

The next morning, Echo felt content for the first time in months. With daylight streaming in through the window, she took a quick shower and spent a few essential minutes looking in the full-length mirror behind the bathroom door.

Now twenty-three years of age, she had been on *Cymbel 3* for over a year. As she cast a critical eye, she realized she had changed. Upon first arriving here, she had been leaner and more muscular due to a life of survival lived over the previous four years. Now her body had filled out, becoming softer and more feminine.

Visits to a local gymnasium several times a week kept her fit, but she took care not to overdo it. She loved that her new, sleeker body drew more attention from the men on the base. Her skin was smoother, the uneven suntan of *Corros* replaced by an all-over shade from a booth. Natural tan was hard to get on this cold world, so she used the same methods as the spacers, who often spent months without sunlight.

The biggest change was not physical. Surrounded by the bustle of the naval base, she had become more street-wise and far less naive. She had lost some of her independence, but her capabilities had grown, giving her more control over her own life.

For the first month after their return, she and Ben had lived in barracks on the base. When he received the promotion to captain, entitling him to better quarters, they moved to an apartment in the married officers' sector, and she began work as an assistant in the Fleet administration office.

It was about then that General Molliner took an interest in her case and arranged her transfer to his personal staff. At first, the situation proved ideal, and when Ben received his new command several weeks later, Echo took it in her stride and knuckled down to the lonely but respectable role as the partner of a serving officer. She made new friends, attended the gym, and did her best to adapt to a new life.

Then news came that Ben was missing, presumed dead. The loss was something she still struggled to deal with and could not accept.

One eyebrow raised, she studied herself in the mirror. The hair was lighter now, and those eyes staring back at her looked less tired than she remembered.

Satisfied her appearance was acceptable, she ran her hands over her flanks and turned to dress. Today's mission was to buy a white suit for her official presentation and a gift for her dinner with the general and his wife. She owed them that much, at least.

That she would receive the highest civilian award was something she could not fully comprehend; she had done only what she considered necessary to survive and to save Ben. Her acceptance for the academy, and in particular the recommendation for officer training, had yet to sink in.

Until five years ago, her prospects had been limited to wife and homemaker in the mining colony where she grew up. On first arriving on *Cymbel 3,* she accepted the role as Ben's partner without hesitation, though they did not marry. With his assumed death, she found herself without purpose, locked in the daily drudge of a well-paid but futureless job. With Ben gone, she moved to a new residence outside the base, and her home was now a small single-bedroom apartment in the town.

Life was lonely without a partner, and whilst the other girls from the office dragged her away for the occasional night out, Echo had not recovered from her loss enough to grasp the opportunities presented. Only once did she allow another man close. He scratched an itch, but no matter how hard she tried, the memory of Ben loomed large in her mind

\* \* \*

In the evening, Echo attended General Molliner's home to spend several hours being congratulated and gushed over by Mrs Molliner. The General's wife was also a dear soul; when Echo departed, she wondered if, after leaving for the academy, she would ever see either of them again.

The following day, with her mentor's dinner behind her, Echo settled down to study for the graduation make-up examination. The file on the data disk had been prepared with special care, and meticulous editing of the information left only what she assumed to be the subjects of the questions in the exam.

It was clear General Molliner did not intend her to fail. At first, his lack of faith incensed her, considering she had studied the same material in school. She realized what an enormous risk he was taking on her behalf and decided to memorize the contents of the cube and then delete it.

# Chapter Three

THE MAIN PARADE GROUND at the naval base bustled with activity. In a small area with temporary seating stands around a low central platform, preparations were underway for the awards ceremony.

The weather was unusually hot for this normally cold world, the sun beating down on the black tarmac of the adjacent airfield and bouncing back in shimmering waves.

Several rows of seats for dignitaries and recipients stood before the dais. Echo took her place as directed, attempting to look as dignified as possible despite the discomfort of wearing the first suit she had ever owned. A few minutes later, a young officer moved to the next row forward.

The man drew attention, exuding confidence in every movement. He stepped up to his seat and locked his steel-blue eyes on Echo's. For a moment too long, he paused, eyes drinking in the young woman before him. An attractive man with blonde, wavy hair, he stood tall and proud, shoulders back and head high, the king of the world. As he sat, he flashed a warm, sincere smile.

*He likes me,* Echo thought.

Clothed in the immaculate dress uniform of Fleet, he wore officer insignia on his epaulets. Echo cursed herself for being seated behind him; he was the first man to pique her interest in months, but once he turned away, his face was no longer visible. With a groan, she settled into her seat, stared at the back of his head, and waited for the ceremony to commence.

The presentations were far too long. Echo coped poorly with public events, breathing a sigh of relief as the actual awards began. She detested formal attire, and while without a doubt the most expensive outfit she had ever owned, the white dress-suit was uncomfortable. A pair of shorts and a shirt or singlet always seemed much more appropriate, except at work.

An odd mixture of body odors and perfumes from numerous people laced the air around her, mingling with the acrid exhaust of ship engines drifting in from the space field. After living so long in the clean, fresh forests of *Corros*, the aromas of civilization assaulted her nose in ways she found distasteful. Sitting in the full sun of midday, even on a normally cold planet like *Cymbel 3*, was not how she preferred to spend her time.

Military honors dominated the proceedings as expected, but Echo heard little of the speeches. Her attention lifted when the man she had been staring at stood and moved towards the dais. From the drone of the microphones, she picked up his name, Marcus Pace, and the fact that he was rated a full captain. He commanded his own ship, like Ben. The award was the Honor-Medal for Bravery.

*Cute*, Eco thought. *Handsome, and brave too.*

"Captain Pace will soon leave here," the awards presenter droned, "to take up a temporary position as instructor at Fleet Naval Academy, where he'll give the benefit of his experiences to future officers while he recovers from recent injuries. Once recovered, he'll return to a new command. We all wish him the best of success at his temporary posting."

Echo's attention peaked as she joined in the round of polite applause. *He's going to the academy. Interesting. If I could just get a closer look at him...*

The only civilian award, Echo's medal, was last on the agenda. She stared at the ground as the presenter rambled about how she had attacked and destroyed a Tollean base single-handed, acquired valuable research, and rescued a Fleet officer.

*Not true,* she thought. Ben took the data—she would have left it.

After receiving the medal, she smiled and stepped down from the dais to thunderous applause from the audience. Several of the more enthusiastic spectators were her chums from the office and gym, but many others whom she did not recognise were also on their feet.

She realized word must have spread of her exploits. Until now, few could fit a face to the stories. Her friends knew, and shielded her to a certain degree, but now—

That evening, sitting in her tiny living room admiring the shiny medal, she sensed her pride returning for the first time since speaking with Molliner. The award was for what she had done personally, for bravery, but she wished they would stop giving her credit for the information retrieved by Ben. The General explained it as "people need heroes," but knowing what the block contained, she wanted nothing more to do with it.

\* \* \*

The spaceport beyond the window looked vast as the bus drove towards the ship that would take Echo to the academy. In her shoulder bag sat a brand new diploma with the highest honors, something she acknowledged as necessary but was indifferent to, considering General Molliner's help.

With the proper texts for study she would have succeeded regardless. Molliner had all but given her the questions, which she acknowledged only from a deep gratitude for the risk taken on her behalf. The same result could have been achieved without his assistance, and that alone made it acceptable.

The tiny craft squatting on the tarmac was not what she expected. It was a shuttle, designed to carry passengers into orbit where they would transfer to a larger transport. Arms crossed, she frowned and gave an audible sigh. *A little small,* she mused. Small spacecraft were not her favorite things.

"Those are quite safe," a masculine voice spoke from nearby.

She turned to face the owner. *Gods,* she thought. *Him.* Before her stood the man she had noticed during the presentation, weeks earlier.

"I remember you," he said. "The medal ceremony, am I right?"

Echo battled to compose herself. "Yes," she replied. At the awards, this man had attracted her, and now he was standing next to her. "Echo. Everyone calls me Echo."

"Pleasure to meet you, Echo. Marc—Marc Pace."

"Captain Marcus Pace, decorated hero."

"No, just Marc. Are you going to Brenton?"

"Yes. The academy, same as you."

31

For a moment, Marc studied her face. "Of course," he said. "The *Corros* girl. You received the Civil Cross. Cinta Bourke, right?"

"Echo!"

The forcefulness of her reply brought a smile to Marc's face. "Echo it is." He turned his attention to the boarding ramp as an officious-looking steward urged them to hurry. "Time to leave. After you." With a small bow, he waved her towards the steps.

Once on board, Echo followed directions to a seat near the front of the cabin, while Marc continued further aft to sit behind her. After a never-ending wait and a directive for passengers to fasten their seatbelts, the shuttle lifted from the tarmac.

The tiny craft lacked external windows, but she could follow its progress on the screen set into the headrest ahead. She had been in space only once, and the video images alone were enough to raise the same feelings of queasiness she experienced when leaving *Corros* a year ago. As the ship rose above the atmosphere, Echo tensed, fighting the unwanted stirrings in the pit of her stomach as she reacted to zero gravity in ways not yet forgotten.

The transport to the academy was not, as expected, a naval vessel. In times of war, military ships serviced the outer worlds, but with the huge losses of the last year, Echo guessed they were needed for front-line duty.

The *Galicia*, an ancient passenger liner from a long-gone era, shared little in common with the craft that once frequented *Corros* or operated from the base on *Cymbel 3*. Incapable of landing on a planet's surface, it depended on shuttles for loading and unloading.

Hanging in space like a giant insect, its main structure was a massive accommodation cylinder rotating around a long backbone. Further back, the spine passed through a second, counter-rotating cargo drum and then a giant, dish-shaped radiation shield. At the stern, grape clusters of spherical tanks filled the spaces between the shield, the reactor unit, and the fusion drive. Heat radiators spread out from this area like giant dragonfly wings. At the extreme forward end, the control deck and docking bay module sprouted a vast array of sensors and communication antennae. The ship was old, almost antique.

Echo followed the approach on the tiny screen, struggling not to lose her breakfast as the shuttle slid through the massive doors of the airlock. She froze as she realized the horrible reality confronting her.

*The center of this thing doesn't rotate.*

To get to her cabin meant floating through the spine of the ship to reach the passenger area. Her only previous experience with weightlessness had been in the military dispatcher she and Ben used to escape from *Corros*. It was not pleasant, and her stomach sank as she anticipated a repeat exercise.

*Tighten up, girl.* Once she began service with Fleet, this would be the norm. She had coped with worse.

Transfer to the liner took only minutes, but it felt like an hour. In the complete absence of gravity, Echo floated forward, pulling herself along a safety line to the elevator. Inside the claustrophobic cubicle, she found herself once again in the company of Captain Pace and a handful of other travelers.

Marc said nothing during the descent, his nose buried in a data pad. Echo kept her peace, trying not to vomit as weight returned to her body. She took a deep breath as the lift began the descent to the lower, outermost level of the drum.

Gravity on the accommodation deck was only one quarter of Earth normal, not enough for complete comfort but sufficient to make sure everything stayed where intended. Echo stood to exit the elevator, stumbled, and lurched to one side.

"Easy," Pace said as he grabbed her arm. "You'll adjust in time. These old ships create gravity by rotation, and it has this nasty effect called Coriolis, caused by inertia and the drum's rotation. Tends to make you drift to one side, but you'll learn to compensate."

He guided her back to her feet. "Watch out for yourself when you move about. You don't weigh much here, but your mass is the same, so if you hit something, it'll leave a bruise."

Echo's rescuer smiled as he left the elevator and disappeared toward the nearest exit. Her face flushed with embarrassment as she steadied herself. *He'll be at the academy,* she thought, *and now he thinks I'm a complete novice … which is exactly what I am.*

"Miss Bourke?" A young man in a white uniform stepped forward, blocking her view of the door through which Marc had departed. She turned her attention to the newcomer. He was young, a steward perhaps in his early twenties, with short black hair and sparkling blue eyes. White teeth flashed as he smiled at Echo.

"Yes?"

"Excellent. David Askin. Allow me to show you to your suite and give you the rundown on how things work … and anything else you need." With another youthful smile, he waved a hand for her to follow, and sauntered towards the door, moving with a strange half-glide Echo took to be the correct way of walking in the strange gravity of this miniature mechanical world.

Emulating his movement to the best of her ability, she followed his bobbing head. At first, she supported herself with a hand against the wall of the corridor, feeling more at ease with each step as her body adjusted.

The cabin, a small, windowless box three meters square, had a sleep-stasis chamber in one corner, above which was a normal, fold-down bunk bed. The rest of the room contained a locker, desk and chair, and a lounge seat. A video screen and many printed notices covered one wall. Thanks to the ship's rapid-fire baggage handling system, her luggage already lay on the bed.

"You have a stateroom," David said, waving his hand across the closet-like room. "Most passengers stay in dorms, or choose to sleep in a pod station all the way. This is because of your status—war hero and all that... "

"No window?" Echo asked, wondering if she had General Molliner to thank for the undoubtedly enormous cost of a private room.

The young man laughed. "No, sorry. You've never been in one of these older liners before, right?"

"No."

"A port would be on the floor. This is a rotating drum, and the floor is the outer shell." He poked a finger downwards. "Outside is down there. The maxi-screen in the lounge gives an exterior view, if you want to see the stars. There's also an observation deck in the forward command module that passengers are permitted to use."

For several minutes, he explained the workings of the ship, pointing out the accommodation map and various sets of posted instructions, including a long list of procedures for the small bathroom hidden behind a narrow door at the rear of the cubicle.

He slapped a hand on the stasis chamber. "The journey will take four weeks, mostly spent cruising through interplanetary space between the gateways. Passengers are always asleep when we pass through a wormhole, but in between, you have a choice. You can sleep the entire trip or be awake between jumps. You can read, write … socialize?" His eyebrows lifted as a smile spread across his face.

*You would love that,* Echo thought. He liked her, his eyes having already thoroughly charted her anatomy. For a moment, she considered the possibilities. *Cute, and about my age.*

The decision to join Fleet represented a watershed for her: With Ben gone, she needed to move on with her life. *Including men,* she thought, looking at the handsome young steward. *No, sorry … you're adorable, but I have someone else in mind.* "Do many passengers stay up?"

"Not many. More experienced travelers tend to mingle, and the military always does. The crew remains on duty throughout, of course."

"Fine. I'll stay awake for now. I have study to do."

"I know all about you. You're famous. I heard you're going to the Academy?"

Echo sighed. "Yes."

"Me as well, I hope. I've applied, and they accept *mature* entrants these days," His back straightened a little on the word 'mature'. "The captain expects I will make it with my experience." For a brief second, he stared at the luggage on the bed. "May I ask a question?"

"Sure, why not?" Echo said, sitting to ease the stress on her unsteady legs.

He looked towards the strange object strapped to Echo's case. "What's that thing?"

"Oh, my crossbow—an ancient weapon. Yes, I know, no weapons on board the ship. I have permission to bring it. It's precious to me." She pointed to the red tag attached to the device.

For a moment, David looked at her, wondering why an attractive, young woman carried an antique bow around with her. He pushed the thought aside and turned to leave.

"Yes, well ... meal times are here." He pointed to a sign over the bunk. "You're at first sitting. Perhaps I'll see you there." With a broad smile, he left.

Alone, Echo debated what she might do for weeks in such a tiny cabin. There were data blocks to study, and then she could sleep the rest of the way, or perhaps get to know Marc Pace. She decided to begin by exploring the ship.

The passenger precinct comprised the outermost level of the rotating drum. Within were all of the accommodation spaces, including private cabins, living, and entertainment areas for the passengers.

Echo found walking in the drum disconcerting. The Coriolis force made a body fall away from the direction of rotation. Stranger still, many of the corridors followed the circumference of the outer wall, creating an impression of being in a curved depression.

For an hour, Echo wandered, familiarizing herself with the layout. Once she had seen enough of the off-white sameness of the hallways, she returned to her cabin and spent time learning to use the bathroom. It did not take long to discover the main function of the diabolical little room: to drive the user insane.

After spending the flight from the planet's surface under stress, she was tired and sweaty. It was good to wash that away, even in a minuscule shower cubicle tailored more to make sure the water stayed where intended than for practicality. Another thing, Echo thought, to which she would need to adjust.

# Chapter Four

THE LARGEST OPEN SPACE on the ship, the function center was a rectangular room stretching lengthwise along the drum. The air hummed with the murmur of voices and the familiar sounds of a public restaurant.

Guided by the wall maps, Echo arrived at the appointed mealtime walking with relative ease in the low gravity, helped by gripping shoes that kept her feet on the carpeted floor surface. At the entrance to the dining area, another steward confronted her.

"Miss Bourke?"

"Does everyone on board know who I am?"

"Just about, Miss. You're a celebrity around here, if you will pardon me for saying. The girl who took out an alien base single-handedly. You'll be at the Captain's table. Follow me, please."

Echo approached the table.

*Oh, Gods … he's here.*

Marc Pace was sitting next to the captain. On her arrival, he stood and withdrew the seat beside his own. She accepted without hesitation. As much as she missed Ben, this man attracted her. *There's no harm in sitting with him at dinner,* she decided.

The meal proved to be more of an ordeal than a pleasure. Captain Henry was a polite and thoughtful host and did his utmost to divert questions, but the other guests left her no choice but to relate the details of her adventures.

The events on *Corros,* and in particular her destruction of the Tollean research base, appeared to be public knowledge. She played down her involvement and gave most of the credit to Ben. Of the stolen data block and the nature of the information thereon, she said nothing.

Across the table, a tall, lean woman with a wolfish look and a suspicious gleam in her eyes peered at Echo. "Is that not a little inconsistent with the award of the Civil Cross?" she asked. "Our young heroine is being modest about her part in the affair, I suspect."

"As is her right," The Captain said. "Captain Pace, tell us about your little adventure at *Borodino.* You received a commendation, I believe."

Echo breathed a sigh of relief and smiled her gratitude as Marc launched into a tale of adventure, of how his ship and two destroyers had been surprised and attacked by a Tollean heavy-cruiser, and how he had disabled the enemy ship by firing on it with a plasma cannon from the disabled wreck of his vessel. The tale was sufficiently 'space opera' to keep the other guests enthralled and away from Echo. His account, spoken by a serving officer, led to general speculation on the war, allowing her to enjoy her meal in peace.

"Are you alright, Cinta?" a voice asked.

Still mildly unsettled from the shuttle trip up, Echo's face was a little flushed. "Yes, I'm fine, thank you. A little queasy, that's all. I'm not used to space travel."

The wolf-lady raised an eyebrow. "You flew from *Corros,* did you not?"

"Yes, but I slept all the way. I haven't been on a ship since."

"Ah, well," Captain Henry interrupted. "Not to worry. You'll be fine after a sleep period. Lieutenant Askin tells me you plan to be awake between jumps."

"Lieutenant Askin?"

The captain nodded towards a nearby table where Echo's young escort from the day before presided over an animated group of diners. "My communications officer. He's applied for Fleet, you know, and they'll accept him on my recommendation. Capable lad—be sorry to lose him."

"Oh, Gods, I thought he was a steward. I was a bit off-hand with him earlier."

"Don't worry, my dear. I suspect he is your biggest admirer."

Echo sighed and slumped back in her seat. The young lieutenant attracted her, but he was no Marc Pace, and neither of them could replace Ben.

Later in the evening, or what served as such on this ship, she decided to retire and excused herself. Marc leapt to his feet and grabbed her chair as she rose.

"Allow me to escort you."

"I'm fine," she said without thinking, and then stopped herself. *Don't be an idiot.* "I mean, that would be wonderful, thank you."

Marc took her arm in his and guided her across the dining room to the exit. "You're achievements have preceded you, I suspect," he said as they left the room.

"Yes … pity."

"I know the problem. It happened to me after the *Borodino* business. Still does, although I expect tonight was more the captain trying to draw the vultures away from you."

"Yes, he's sweet."

"Which is your door?"

"It's the royal suite, along there."

"Ah, right. The standard three-meter square shoe-box."

"Yes. I expected a window. I didn't realize they don't have them."

"Not on this old boat. Nothing to see but stars, but no huge loss. You're lucky you're not economy; they're all asleep in pod storage on the level above us."

Outside her cabin, Echo inserted her key-card and then turned to study Marc's face, wondering if he was hoping for an invitation. *Should I?* He was a beautiful man, and she craved his company, but discretion warned her she should get to know him better first.

*You only just met Ben when you slept with him*, the contrary voice in her head interrupted.

"Thank you for showing me back," she said. "The corridors are confusing." She had known the way, but appreciated the attention.

"My pleasure. Until breakfast?"

"Yes…" Echo gazed into his eyes as he stood in the corridor. This was harder than she expected. This man attracted her, but she still thought of Ben.

*He went missing months ago—he's dead.*

The base office had assured her Ben's chances of still being alive were zero. No trace of his vessel was found on any charted planet. If the ship was derelict in space, hope for survivors had passed long ago. The search, minimal because of the war, had been abandoned, and General Molliner had advised that she should get on with her life.

Ben's loss was the whole point of her application to the academy, and deep inside, she still hoped he was alive. In

Fleet, she might find him. She had no chance sitting in an office.

"Would you like to come in?"

"I'd love to," Marc said, stepping back, "but I promised to meet the captain for a tour of the bridge in a few minutes. This is an ancient tub, but he's proud of her. It's a long voyage and I'm sure I'll run into you again ... soon?" He flashed a warm, friendly smile.

"Yes ... I expect so," Echo said, deflated after having struggled for the courage to ask him in.

"Until later." Marc smiled again and glided away along the corridor. Echo waited until he vanished around the nearest corner, sad that he had turned down her offer. Another part of her was glad: it would have been a betrayal of the love to which she still clung. After closing the door, she sat at the computer terminal in her room and typed in a search string.

*'Marcus-Pace-Borodino.'*

\* \* \*

Marc returned to the dining room, wondering what Echo thought of him. Such a pity she chose to come on this particular voyage, he thought. Such a waste. Still, no reason I can't have fun with her.

He already knew about Ben Teague, and the minute he arrived on board, he had researched the girl's name. He did not doubt she still harbored feelings for Teague, but the man was out of the picture now. That, Marc knew as an absolute fact.

A shipboard affair appealed to him, but was problematical. He did not need a long-term relationship at present, and besides, she would be just another conquest. Regardless, the chance for anything serious to develop was never going to happen. That was also sure.

*   *   *

After the sleep period, the passenger section's dimmed lights returned to full strength. Echo woke to a knock on her door. Scrambling from the bunk, she snatched a robe from the floor and wrapped it around herself.

*Gods,* she thought, rushing to the door. *That has to be Marc.*

Lieutenant Askin stood in the corridor. "Morning, Miss Bourke. I wondered if you would like a guided tour following breakfast."

"I ... um ... had a quick look around yesterday, thanks."

David raised an eyebrow. "No, I don't mean the accommodation section. Captain Henry suggested I give you the grand tour; most passengers don't rate that, but you're a war hero. You're invited up to the bridge, and then we can check out the rest of the ship. I can show you the inner decks in the drum, the engine rooms, and the service bays in the command module. You might find it helpful since you're going to the academy. You'll get an idea of the workings of these older vessels and a chance to adjust to weightlessness."

*How,* Echo wondered, *did he know I can't handle zero gravity? Am I that obvious?* Against her better judgment—she had intended to study—she accepted the offer, then showered, dressed, and headed to the dining area.

Marc waited at the captain's table, greeting her with his usual smile. The captain was absent, and few other passengers or crew were in sight.

44

She took the seat next to him. "Doesn't anybody eat breakfast?"

Marc glanced around at the empty tables. "Not on the first morning, usually," he said. "Most of them overdo the departure evening meal and end up paying for it the next day. You need to keep meals light on these old centrifuge buckets. You're doing well, considering you have no flight experience."

"At least the wolf lady isn't here. I think she hates me."

"Ah, yes, Lady Amanda Britton. Don't mind her; it's an act. She treats people the way she thinks someone of her standing should, regardless of whether she approves of them or not. I suspect she likes you."

"How can you tell?"

"She's my aunt. She's traveling on to *Al-Kuduk* to see old friends—came on board after us."

Echo dropped her eyes to the tabletop. "Gods, I called your aunt the 'wolf lady'. I'm so sorry. That was unforgivable."

"Don't concern yourself. Amanda would think it hilarious. She's a dear once you get to know her." Marc leaned closer. "What do you have planned for this wake period?"

"Lieutenant Askin is giving me the grand tour of the ship. Maybe I'll check out the gymnasium later and have a swim. Then I have to study." At that moment, her breakfast arrived, so she pretended to concentrate on eating.

At the end of the breakfast session, David Askin stepped up to the table and, with a patronizing smile in Marc's direction, helped Echo from her chair. Once outside the dining room, he led her towards the elevator, rambling on about the ship's facilities as they walked.

"There'll be a drill this evening, so you'll find out where your nearest lifeboat is. In an extreme emergency where you can't reach a boat, we also have emergency pods that will get you to a planet's surface or keep you alive in space for a week. You'll learn about them at the academy."

The first stop on the tour was the bridge deck. For half an hour, Captain Henry gushed over Echo, showing her the various control stations and the functions of the ship while Lieutenant Askin waited to one side. He grinned as she floated back to him. She felt herself warming to this pleasant young man. Every smile lit up his face with warmth and familiarity.

"This is my station," he said, pointing to a console behind the helm. "I keep us in touch with the rest of the known universe. Not much to do when we're outside occupied systems, so I do backup in other positions. Each officer here is multi-talented, of course."

"I'm sure they are," Echo replied. "I owe you an apology. Yesterday, I was blunt with you. I thought you were a steward."

"No problem." He gave an offhand wave, grinning as he turned toward the exit hatch. "It happens a lot."

From the bridge, he led her aft through the central spine corridor of the ship, past the elevators to a point where several short passages exited.

"Those lead to the storage holds," he said. "They're locked during the voyage."

Echo peered into an access way. At the far end, a soldier sat tethered to the floor, a laser rifle in his lap.

"Don't ask what that's about," David said. "Four of those guys are on board, and one is always in front of that hatch. There's something important in the cargo, I expect."

"Like what?"

"No idea. Pace knows though. He spends a lot of time with the Captain, and I saw him heading along here last watch."

David floated further along the corridor towards the ship's stern. In the engine room, he poked into every corner and cavity, explaining the purpose of each space and device. By the time they had covered the whole module, Echo's head spun with information she would never remember. At least she had part-mastered the techniques of moving around in zero gravity and was enjoying herself more.

"You know everything about this ship, don't you?" she said as they stepped into the service areas.

"I grew up on it. My father was the first officer before he died, and with no mom, I spent most of my life with him. I've seen every cranny in this thing." David turned into a toilet cubicle and patted a panel on the wall.

"Take this, for instance. It's a hatch, although you would never know to look at it. It leads to the space between the inner and outer hull shells. There are service bays down there that nobody ever sees. I used them as a hideout when I was tiny. I could disappear for hours, days if I wanted, but I never did—always came back up for meals."

The tour ended with the areas of the accommodation module that Echo had not yet visited. Besides the upper crew and pod storage decks, there was a small theater where, according to the official schedule, members of the crew put on an occasional live show for the edification of the passengers. David doubted they would bother this time around with so few on board.

After lunch, Echo went to the gymnasium, where an adjacent room contained a pool. Discovered on her first investigation, it had come as something of a blessing. Swimming, or at least being in water, was a passion.

Too small for proper exercise, the facility served mainly as a comfort to passengers, being little more than a huge bath with seating around the edge below the water level. A solid cover slid from one side to contain the liquid when, for any reason, the drum slowed or stopped, losing the centrifugal gravity.

On her home world, the convention had been to swim nude, but here she was unsure of the customs. She compromised with a black, two-piece costume, enough to preserve modesty and a little mystery.

Upon entering the room, she found Marc Pace waiting. Careful to mention her intentions earlier, she had hoped he would be there. He sat on the far side of the pool, leaning against the wall.

"I wondered if you would be here," she said, approaching the pool.

"I love this place. This is a real luxury in space. Care to join me?"

Echo shrugged off the robe and basked in Marc's gaze as he ran his eyes over her almost naked form, then eased herself into the water. As she sat, he dropped from the edge and floated across, settling into the seat beside her.

"You won't find this on Fleet ships," he said. "Strictly for passenger vessels."

"I don't think I could live without being able to take a dip now and then," she said.

"In the service it will be more then, and less now—better accept it."

Half an hour of small talk later, Echo announced she had work to do and climbed out, reaching for a towel from a nearby alcove. Marc joined her and dried himself. "Please, allow me to walk you back to your cabin."

*Perfect,* she thought as she donned her robe. "Thank you. That will be nice."

Once outside the cabin, she inserted the key into the lock and turned to Marc. He was handsome without question and well built like all spacers, but he wasn't Ben. Still, something about him drew her in—she felt lightheaded whenever in his presence.

It was not only the sound of his voice, nor his appearance, as attractive as he was. She sensed a chemistry drawing them together and a strong feeling that he understood what she wanted and needed.

She locked eyes with him for a long moment.

"Care to join me?" This time, she knew what his answer would be.

"Yes, I'd love to, but I shouldn't. You said you had work to do?"

"Oh, for the Gods' sake." Echo grasped the front of his robe and pulled him into the cabin.

\* \* \*

Sometime later, her eyes closed, Echo luxuriated in the warm water of the shower as it ran over her skin. Without warning, thoughts of Ben surged into her mind. She needed that contact, but knew she had been unfaithful to the man with whom she had been through so much.

The annoying voice at the back of her consciousness, something she heard less often now, made its usual pitch. *He's dead, gone. The general said so, and he never lied to you. You need to move on with your life.*

*I do,* Echo acknowledged. Marc was rather delicious, the most gorgeous man she had met since her partner's disappearance. Reserved and sometimes distant, but always a gentleman, he had a mystery about him. And that voice—

His effect on her was not like Ben's, but the circumstances were different. She was not fighting for survival here and did not need rescue. In addition, Marc was not her first real partner, and she had become much wiser in the last year.

# Chapter Five

ECHO WOKE WITH A start, unsure of whether she was dreaming or not. It took only seconds to realize she was lying in her stasis capsule, the lid wide open. David Askin loomed over her, a strained expression on his face.

"Come on," he urged, shaking her by the shoulders. "Wake up—now!"

Echo struggled to sit. "Waa… I'm awake. What's wrong? How long have I been asleep?"

"Three weeks. You need to get up."

"What? I was only supposed to sleep for a couple of hours, wasn't I?"

"Long story. The ship's been attacked. I'll explain later, but I'm taking you to a safe place first."

"Who … the Tolleani?" she asked, climbing from the pod. She grabbed the nearest clothes—her much-loved cargo shorts, a singlet top, and sneakers—then dressed and allowed David to guide her from the room. Instead of heading for an elevator, he scrambled into a nearby maintenance shaft, urging her to follow as he climbed towards the central spine of the ship.

"What's happening?" Echo rushed to keep up, trying not to show panic. "Who's attacking us?"

"A pirate ship—human, not Tollean—stopped us a week ago after the passengers went to sleep for the wormhole transit. It was sitting in front of the gateway. They forced us to stop under threat of attack. This ship isn't armed, and the bandits have a destroyer. We couldn't prevent them from boarding."

Echo struggled up the ladder behind her rescuer. "Where are we going?"

"Somewhere safe. These guys want the cargo, whatever it is, and I doubt they intend to leave any witnesses. I'm not letting them take you." David reached up to undo a hatch at the top of the shaft. "I'll hide you and see what I can do about getting us out of here. Come on, we don't have much time. They're waking up everyone as we speak."

Once in the corridor, he made sure nobody was in sight, then took Echo by the hand, turned, and launched himself toward the stern. As they passed through, she stole a glance along the guarded passageway. The soldier was gone, the door to the cargo bay open.

Inside the engineering module, David led her to a maintenance compartment. He pressed a hand against the wall to release a hidden latch and then pushed to reveal a wide shaft containing more ladder rungs.

"In you go," he said. "I'll be right behind you, after I close this panel again."

Echo entered the duct headfirst, grasped the top rung, and pulled herself downwards before twisting through a short access-way into a larger space. David floated in behind her.

"This is a service bay below the main engineering deck, another place I used to play when I was a kid. No one except the crews of these old ships knows about these, so you'll be safe here. I'll be back soon." Without hesitation, he pushed himself towards the exit.

"Wait. You can't leave me down here. What's going on, for the Gods' sake?"

"I'm sorry, Echo, but please have patience. I won't be long." David disappeared back up the shaft. Seconds later, she heard the panel click closed.

The refuge was little more than a narrow gap between the hull shell and the interior deck. Structural framing covered every surface, with dozens of pipes and electrical cable tiers running along the walls and ceiling. A single light, switched on by David as they entered, glowed at the center of the cavity. A faint breath of cool air betrayed a ventilator somewhere behind the piping. On one wall sat a small computer terminal.

"What in the Hells am I supposed to do here?" Echo wondered aloud. "What's going on?" She drifted to a corner and wedged herself against a convenient upright. With no choice but to wait, an overwhelming sense of dread began to grow, thoughts both fearful and confused battling for contention in her mind. If David did not return, she had no idea what to do next.

She had barely secured herself when another click came from above, and her rescuer reappeared. He was wearing an emergency vacuum suit and pushed another, complete with helmet and backpack unit, in front of him.

"Put this on now. These guys might void the ship to space to make their job easier. Back soon." With a quick grin, he vanished up the duct again, leaving Echo to pull herself into the suit. Another fifteen minutes passed before he returned.

"Damn it, David," Echo snapped. "Tell me what's happening."

"Sorry." He pulled himself down to the deck beside her. "The rebels stopped us three weeks ago and forced us to reroute through a series of wormholes until we arrived here. They wouldn't let us wake the passengers, so you slept through the whole thing. We're in orbit around an unknown planet. Here, come and see this."

David floated across to the terminal and switched on the monitor, tapping the screen until a clear picture appeared. The image looked across the outer ship's hull towards the night-side surface of a dark world. There were no visible lights, indicating the planet was devoid of cities. Between the *Galicia* and the planet sat the long, sinister shape of another spacecraft.

"The bandits' ship," David said. "A Fleet destroyer. Where the bastards got it I don't know, but we can't compete. It can reduce us to atoms in seconds."

Echo stared dumbstruck at the other vessel. On its side was a line of faint digits, along with the roundel of the Terran space force, both still visible despite obvious attempts to remove them. She had seen that number before, on the day of the ship's commissioning.

"It's Ben's," she whispered, tears forcing their way into her eyes.

"Ben? Your Ben?"

"Yes." Echo strained to see the image through watery eyes. "What are pirates doing with it?"

For a few seconds, David remained silent. "Yes, well," he said, "the point is they have it and are using it to hijack us. At this moment, they're waking everyone and moving them to the lifeboats, maybe to take them down to the planet. I

54

don't know what they intend to do, but it can't be anything good. With your sleep-pod empty, I'm hoping they'll think you're in a shuttle already, and won't worry about you."

"What about you? Won't they miss you?"

"Not yet. They needed us to pilot the ship here, so until now I've had a little freedom to move about. With both of us hidden, they might overlook me in the confusion."

"Where's Marc Pace?"

"I'm not sure. I think they're holding him somewhere with those soldiers. Haven't seen him since they boarded us."

Echo slumped back into her corner, unsure whether David's actions were wise or not. "Why did you come for me?" she asked. He did not reply, his face turning bright red as he looked away.

*He's in love with me...*

\*   \*   \*

An hour later, she was alone again, watching the image on the service monitor and waiting for David to return. The lifeboats had departed for the planet's surface minutes earlier, and now Ben's ship was moving away. As it left, David floated into the bay.

"Come on," he said. "We have to go now." With a firm grip on her arm, he urged her towards the shaft.

Echo resisted. "Tell me what's going on or I'm not going anywhere."

"The bandits have abandoned the ship. They offloaded the crew, passengers, and cargo, and now you and I are the only ones still on board. I don't know if they've missed us yet, but the ship's in a deteriorating orbit. We'll hit the atmosphere in about three hours and crash into one of those oceans down there, if we don't burn on the way down. They don't intend to leave any evidence."

"Shit." Without hesitation, Echo ceased her defiance and followed. She knew little about spacecraft, but understood a ship of this type could not survive a descent from space into an atmosphere. "How do we get out?"

"Guess. Come, I'll show you. I'm sorry, but you won't enjoy this."

In a secluded corner of the engineering module was a hatch to another service bay containing a number of small domes set in the floor. Each dome had an open hatch at the top. It took Echo only seconds to realize these were the small emergency pods David had mentioned earlier. Without pause, he floated across to a console and began tapping at the screen.

"First off, we launch a backtrack beacon."

"Sorry?"

"The bandits forced us to reroute through several wormholes. They don't know it, but the auto-navigator recorded every course alteration. The beacon will travel back along the return path until it reaches a known, civilized system or detects a Terran ship, then send out a distress signal. Fleet can use the data it carries to find this world. There —done."

From beneath the stern of the ship, a small drone detached and drifted away to a predetermined distance before powering towards the last gateway. Satisfied, David led Echo to one of the escape units and motioned for her to climb through the hatch and into the seat.

"These only carry one person," he explained, "so we go down in separate pods."

Echo's stomach jumped into her throat.

"Don't stress over it," he added. "These little beauties are automatic; they're programmed to detect the nearest habitable planet and take us down to the surface."

Echo swallowed hard, trying to ignore the pounding she could feel in her temples. "We can't leave any other way?"

"No. This ship will burn in a few hours, and these are our only way off. The bad guys took all the lifeboats and jettisoned most of the pods. They missed the ones here in engineering. This room is not obvious, and they must have been in a hurry."

"Why would they do that?"

"I guess they worked out we were still here and didn't want to waste time. It would take too long to search, so they arranged for us to burn. Lucky for us, they're not very efficient."

"Is it safe? Their base is down there, isn't it?"

"Yes, but we don't have a choice. The pods will locate dry land and take us close to any detectable civilization, but we have to risk it. It's not the best option, but if we landed in an uninhabited wilderness, we might be dead in days anyway."

"I'm pretty good with uninhabited wilderness," Echo mumbled, struggling to control the shaking in her legs as she clambered into the escape pod. Sweat beaded on her brow as she realized the tiny craft was little more than a transparent bubble. "What about you?"

"I'll take another. They communicate automatically, so we'll land near each other. Once you're down, fire one of those flares, there, and I'll find you."

"David, I..." Before Echo finished the sentence, the overhead hatch slammed shut, and she sat alone in what she was convinced would be her coffin. Strapped in tightly, she took a deep breath as, without warning, the hull opened and the pod dropped, floating away from the doomed ship.

She closed her eyes, clutching the edges of the seat until her hands ached. She had never been in space unprotected. David had assured her she was safe inside the resilient emergency vehicle, but the knowledge did little to ease the growing terror.

Eyes open again, she looked at her transport. The pod consisted almost entirely of a transparent bubble. At the rear, a solid section carried the small rocket motor now driving her planet-wards, and at the front, a small, cylindrical nose structure protruded.

The inside of the vehicle was empty except for the seat and a console on a stem rising from the floor between Echo's legs. Echo tried not to touch it; the craft was supposed to be automatic, pre-programmed to take her down without interference.

Straining to look around the aft engine unit, she searched for David. He promised he would be close behind, but there was no sign of another pod. Not even the space-liner was visible as it tore away from her in the opposite direction. Far below, the dark, unknown world was drawing closer.

Echo closed her eyes again. Aware she was in a tiny bubble over which she had no control, she battled to fight back fear as the vehicle hurtled towards the dawn line on the planet below. It approached the atmosphere at a shallow angle, short puffs of gas from small jets guiding it to an area predetermined to be safe and dry.

Unable to cope with the uncertainty, Echo forced herself to take another look. She was flying lower, the planet now filling the horizon; a blue-gray vastness stretched in every direction.

*Water. That's the ocean down there. This thing will end up in the water, and I'll drown.*

Nowhere was there any sign of land. She gripped the armrests tightlyr as the surface of the bubble shimmered with heat.

*Oh, Gods, I'm hot. I'm going to burn.*

The sound of heavy breathing filled her ears; her body trembled as she waited for what would surely be a painful death. The moments passed with a cold detachment as her mind retreated into a state of disconnected awareness. It was as if she were not there, a mere casual observer watching from a distance.

She recalled what she had read about atmospheric re-entry in the data she was studying for the academy. The friction from air particles would heat the vehicle to white-hot —the thought did not help. She wondered if the thin, transparent material could withstand the high temperature.

*David said it was safe…*

The pod rotated, turning her away from the direction of travel. With a jolt, the jet fired again. Now facing backwards, Echo saw a small glowing pinpoint in the distance; she prayed it was David following behind.

Farther away, now well around the curve of the planet but still visible, a larger object flashed. She realized she was looking at the *Galicia* reflecting the light of the nearby star as it vanished beyond the horizon.

A loud thud shook the little craft. From a point forward of the engine, a metal disk composed of intersecting plates expanded behind the passenger compartment. Echo wondered if it was a heat shield.

Most of the figures on the console display meant nothing, but a few were clear. One, labeled 'Mach', read 'three-point-nine'.

*Gods ... am I going that fast?*

A second figure, showing the surface temperature of the bubble, was rising, already reading several hundred degrees centigrade; safe inside, Echo was just warm. Her body trembled beyond control as she wiped the perspiration from her stinging eyes, then took a deep breath and watched the speed reduce as the vehicle slowed under the influence of the rocket motor.

Pushed beyond its limits, her stomach took control; turning to one side, she dry retched. She had not eaten through weeks of hibernation and had nothing to relinquish, but it made little difference.

With a glance, she realized she was descending through clouds. *I'll drown,* she thought again, struggling for breath as the pod punched through the white haze.

Below the cloud, a coastline stretched away in a line of sandy beaches. Small blasts from the attitude jets forced the vessel to drift sideways, plunging lower at what Echo still thought to be deadly velocity. Her head spun as she began to lose consciousness, her lungs laboring hard and her breaths deep. She shook her head and fought to maintain awareness.

The craft continued to descend, slower now but still moving at breakneck speed. At a predetermined height, a parachute emerged from the front cylinder, causing the pod to slow further.

On her back with the massive canopy stretched above, Echo prayed she would not break every bone in her body on landing. Seconds later, she blacked out. With a deafening roar, the main jet sprang to life once more, balancing the little ship on a column of fire as it settled towards the surface.

*  *  *

Echo opened her eyes. The rescue vehicle was down. It had landed while she was unconscious—not a bad thing, she thought—and now rested nose up in an area covered by short, spiky vegetation.

Close by, sand ridges rose to higher coastal dunes, showing she was near the beaches she had seen earlier. Hopefully, David was down and not far away. For several minutes she lay still, thankful to be still breathing.

"How the hell do I get this undone?" She struggled to uncouple the restraining belts that kept her secure during the descent, as shaking hands made it hard to work the release on the buckles. Despite the loss of consciousness, the last hour had been the most traumatic of her life; her heart still beat frantically and her lips trembled, her mind numb with shock.

She reached above her head and undogged the hatch, then scrambled out of the bubble. Once on the ground, she slumped to the blackened sand. Her body shivered, and tears flooded from her eyes.

# Chapter Six

A YELLOW SUN SHONE high in a clear blue sky as Echo picked herself up and examined her surroundings. With no knowledge of where the pod landed, she had no idea which way to go. Nor did she know anything of the planet's direction of rotation. She could not tell from the sun's movement whether she was in the northern or southern hemisphere. Unsure what to do next, she took off the pressure suit and threw it back into the pod.

Behind her, a line of sand hills marked the nearby coastline. That was good; the long sandy beaches offered a path if necessary. Humans tended to inhabit inlets and rivers, and if civilization was nearby, following the coastline was the best way to find it, but which direction?

Conversely, this might have been a mining or forestry planet. The majority of colony worlds started that way, so the towns would be close to the ore or timber, coastal or otherwise. On her home world, the mines were near the sea, as were the settlements, and connecting roads followed the shoreline. That did not mean the same was true here.

The surrounding area was tufted dune-grass growing in sand, with a few small copses of stunted vegetation scattered nearby. A short distance further inland, a line of trees stretched away on either side, beyond a band of low scrub.

With a deep sigh, Echo climbed back into the pod to retrieve the signal pistol David pointed out before launching her into space. She prayed he had followed her down and was somewhere nearby.

With a hand held up through the hatch, she fired a flare. High above, it ignited into a brilliant white star, a clear beacon even in daylight. David would see it for sure, she thought, climbing back down to the sand.

In the hope of finding emergency equipment or supplies of any kind, she cast an eye over the pod. The interior of the bubble contained nothing, and there was no sign of hatches or lids on the blackened exterior of the pod's aft section.

While she stood gazing out towards the dunes, something caught her attention. Farther along the coast, perhaps a half kilometer distant, a pinpoint of light climbed into the bright sky, drifting on a column of smoke.

*Yes,* she thought. David was close and alive. He would come to her, so she decided to stay put and wait. The flare pistol contained two more rounds to guide him, if necessary.

A loud click sounded, and Echo spun to face the noise. A man stood only meters away, a strange weapon in his hands, pointed at her stomach.

The device looked familiar—Echo had seen something like it once before, over a year ago. She and Ben had spent time hiding in a deserted naval base on *Corros* while he repaired their escape ship. In an old cabinet, she had discovered what he described as an 'antique projectile weapon' designed to fire small, metal slugs.

Careful not to make any aggressive moves, she raised her hands in supplication. Old or not, all weapons could kill.

"Hello," she said. "Can you lower that thing, please?"

"Jest stay where ye are," The man spoke standard Tantallic, the prime language of the Federation worlds, but his words sounded clipped and coarse, the accent stronger than any she had heard before. He looked like a vagrant, his clothes old, worn, and grimy, and his hair dirty and unkempt.

The wild, desperate glare in his eyes frightened Echo. *Was he safe, or even sane?* He scratched at several days' growth shading his face, then flicked the rifle barrel to one side, urging her to move.

"I can't leave here," she said. "I'm waiting for someone." No sooner had the words left her mouth than the gun fired with a deafening bang and a fountain of dirt puffed from the ground beside her.

"Put yer hands behind yer head and walk that way," he said, nodding his head towards the nearby trees.

The loud explosion shook Echo, so she decided not to take any chances; the man did not behave in a manner at all friendly. She obeyed without further hesitation and shuffled in the direction indicated, dragging her feet in the sand to leave a sign for David. The stranger moved in behind to follow at a short distance, his rifle raised and aimed.

At the scrub line, a worn, sandy trail led away towards the trees. Echo followed the track, neither looking at nor speaking to her assailant. As long as the weapon remained aimed at her she would avoid antagonizing him.

Whenever the path divided, he directed her in his rough, uneducated voice until their journey stopped at a grassy clearing containing a small, run-down cabin.

A sandy road emerged from the nearby trees and ended at the structure. Beneath a tarpaulin next to the dwelling sat an ancient vehicle of a type Echo did not recognize. Through a gap in the vegetation, she saw what appeared to be crop fields.

*This is 'detectable civilization'?* she wondered. Her captor, obviously a farmer, must have seen the pod descend. She prayed he was not with the bandits.

Something sharp prodded her in the back. The man had closed up behind and motioned for her to walk to the cabin door and enter. Once inside, he shoved her towards an old, worn sofa on one side of the main room of the building. She slumped onto the seat, remaining motionless.

"Ye come down from space, yeah?" he asked.

"Yes."

"The bosses are after ye. They sez on the radio to watch out for anyone and tell them quick. Reckon there's rewards."

Echo sighed. The bandits had known all along she and David were missing, and rather than waste time searching for them, they has set the liner to plunge into the atmosphere, to kill them. The ship was of no value to them, nor were human lives. "Are you going to tell them I'm here?"

"Done that already, when I sees ye come down. They'll be on their way now."

*Shit.* Echo thought, looking around the room. There was only one door to the outside, and her captor was between her and it, gun in hand.

"You didn't have to turn me in," she said in her most seductive voice. *If you can't beat them, work around them.* "I'm not dangerous."

The man did not respond. For half an hour, he stood by the door staring at her, his rifle held firmly in both hands. He was waiting for the 'bosses' to arrive, and Echo realized the longer she waited, the less her chances of escape.

There was only one possibility. The farmer had not taken his eyes off her since their arrival at the farmhouse, his attention not on her face but on her breasts and groin. She wondered if he lived alone and how long he had been without female company. This, she thought, was her way out.

With a hand on one breast, she stretched the thin fabric of the singlet to show the slightest bump of a nipple.

*Come on, girl. You need to escape ... you can do this.* "We have to wait for your bosses," she said, "so why don't you come over here. I promise I won't try anything." She prayed this man was as simple as he seemed.

He stood fixated, as she lifted her singlet up and over her head, threw it on the floor and stood, hands resting on her hips in a casual, seductive manner. Startled by the sudden and unexpected movement, he stepped forward, raising the barrel of his gun.

"What ye up to?" His eyes remained glued to her chest.

"Just making myself comfortable. I feel like company and you're the only man around here. Interested?" Sitting again, she spread her legs and slid a finger down her belly and under the band of her shorts, hoping the blatant display would suffice to throw him off guard.

Her captor's eyes grew wide. The sight of a beautiful young woman half-naked on his couch left him defenseless. Unable to resist, he rested the rifle against the wall by the door, took a quick glance through the window, and then moved closer. A broad smile spread across his face, revealing a mouth full of brown and ill-cared-for teeth.

As he approached, she closed her knees together; to reach her, he would have to straddle them. She slid forward, spreading her arms wide as if making herself ready for him.

Soon, he stood right where she wanted him, legs apart, looking down at her. She raised a foot between his knees, forcing him to separate them further to move closer. As he leaned in he placed a hand on her breast and grinned.

*Oh, Gods*, she thought. *Please make this work.*

In a single, smooth motion, she brought her leg up hard, driving her shin into his testicles. As if hit by an electric shock, her captor jerked away. A loud wail escaped his lips as his face contorted in extreme agony. He stumbled back and collapsed on the floor, both hands grasping his tortured manhood.

Echo leapt from the couch, shot across the room and grabbed the rifle by the barrel, swinging the wooden butt hard against the side of her captor's head, knocking him unconscious with a single blow.

*God's, I can't believe I did that. Thanks, Dad.* Her long-dead father always worried that one of the miners on *Corros* might someday decide to take advantage. Long ago, when she was still a teenager, he taught her how to take down a man. The lesson had not been used until now, but she never forgot it.

"Shit!" she cursed, dropping to her knees beside the unconscious body. "You're not dead, are you?" She felt his neck until she found a slow but steady pulse. "I'm so sorry, I don't make a habit of treating men this way, but I can't let you give me to the bad guys."

Retrieving her top, she re-dressed. The full reality of her actions hit her; this man was twice her size, hard and muscular from long hours of laboring in the fields, and one kick to the genitals had reduced him to nothing.

Never before had she done anything like that to a man, and she could not believe it now. In all likelihood, he was only a lonely farmer with no choice but to turn her in for fear of repercussions. Using his loneliness against him was not something to be proud of, but survival came first.

She moved to restrain him, but decided against it. Unless someone found him soon, the unfortunate man might die of starvation or thirst: she wanted to escape, not become a murderer.

The rifle in hand, she wrenched the door open, intending to return to the dunes and once there, to locate David. With luck, he would be at the pod when she returned.

The sunlight blinded her as she stepped through the doorway. She stopped short, realizing she was not alone. Three men stood in a line, leaning against the side of a military truck she had not heard arrive. They were not soldiers, or at least wore no uniforms, but there was no doubting who they were.

"Put the antique on the ground, Missy," one man ordered, his weapon pointed straight at Echo's belly. "It'll probably blow up in your face anyway. I have orders not to harm you, but accidents happen ... don't they?"

Echo stared at her new captors. With no choice but to obey, she placed the gun on the ground and raised her hands.

The new arrival looked past her towards the cabin. "So, what did you do with old Erin? Kill the poor bastard, did you?"

"No, he's fine. A little unconscious is all."

"Lucky for you," the pirate said. "The boss doesn't like our farmers being damaged." Without another word, he stepped forward, picked up the old rifle, and shoved her towards the back of the truck. As she climbed onto the canvas-covered tray, a pained voice came from a shape huddled in the dim interior.

"Echo?"

"David?" She crawled to the inert figure propped against the side. "Are you all right?

"Yes. A bit worked over, that's all—maybe because I tried to resist. No serious damage, though." With a grimace, he raised himself into a sitting position. Echo reached across and placed a hand to his cheek.

"I'm so glad you're alive."

"You missed me?" A wide but pained grin spread across his face. "Did you enjoy the ride down?"

"Oh, yes. For that, I will never forgive you. You might've warned me."

"You would never have got into the pod if I had. Those things are designed to save lives in an emergency, not to give a pleasant experience. I *am* sorry though."

"Okay, fair enough. You're still not forgiven." Echo slumped down beside him. "Do you have any idea where these guys are taking us?"

"No. Just after I found your pod they came from nowhere and grabbed me. I've been in here ever since."

"Are they the ones who took over the ship?"

"I expect so, or with them at least. I don't recognize anyone but it seems logical. They didn't kill us, so I'm guessing we'll be joining our fellow crew members and passengers soon."

"Hardly worth all the trouble, was it?"

"Yes, it was. We got the backtrack beacon away—that's something in our favor."

Minutes later the vehicle roared to life and began a slow crawl over the lumpy sand-track serving as an entrance to the farm. After a while, the constant lurching eased as the truck turned along a better road.

The canopy was canvas over a steel frame. Echo climbed back to her feet and steadied herself against the side of the enclosure. At a gap in the covering, she hooked her fingers through and strained to see out.

They were moving across a forest-covered hillside, high above the ocean. The trees crowded close, breaking occasionally to show a glimpse of water but otherwise limiting the view to a blur of green.

After an hour of travel they left the coast and turned inland, climbing higher to a plateau covered with sparser vegetation. Huge structures Echo recognized as the pitheads of underground mines dotted the surrounding landscape, interspersed with gigantic mounds of mine tailings. She had guessed right; this was a mining planet like her home world, but older.

Without warning the truck jerked to a halt. The doors at the rear swung open and a guard ordered Echo and Ben to disembark. They were in a large, chain-wire-fenced compound containing numerous buildings. In front of the vehicle, a multi-storied, gray, concrete-block building stood before a tall and obsolete looking pithead.

The complex was larger, and much older than the ones on *Corros*. The bandits were organized and numerous, judging by the number moving around the compound.

Again, Echo wondered where this world was. Beyond the fence and about a half a kilometer distant, she could see what were either spacecraft or aeroplanes. The landing field was there and so, she expected, was Ben's destroyer.

Once again his fate weighed into her thoughts. It was unthinkable he would have anything to do with this, so it made sense his ship was captured the same as hers. If he still lived, he would be somewhere nearby. Deep inside, a spark of hope flickered, but dimly. Most likely the rebels had killed him.

"I think they want us to go in there," David said, dragging her attention away from the airfield. Several men stood around them with weapons raised, leaving a clear path to the building.

Once inside, the guards ushered them to an empty room and locked the door behind them. Echo dashed to the only window and looked through. A guard stood outside, but the visible part of the compound was otherwise deserted. She turned back to David, who had slumped onto the floor beside the door, and shook her head.

"That went well," he said.

"At least we're alive," Echo replied. "We don't know what happened to everyone else. They could be dead."

# Chapter Seven

NOBODY ENTERED THE ROOM while daylight lasted, leaving the captives alone with their thoughts. This did not surprise Echo, but desperate to learn what was going on, she tried hard not to become morose.

Her original motivation for this journey had been to enter the academy and begin a new life, to make up for the years lost on *Corros* and perhaps recover from the loss of Ben. Never giving up all hope, she refused to accept his death; the thought he might still be alive and on this planet smoldered in her brain.

The destroyer she had seen in space was his—that was certain. Those same identification numbers were visible on the hull when Ben invited her as his partner to the ship's commissioning ceremony.

Somehow, the pirates had taken the vessel intact, and presumably the crew with it. There was every chance they were dead, but hope remained that they survived and were prisoners somewhere nearby. Echo had not planned on being captured, but discovering what happened to the man she loved would make it worthwhile. As daylight faded, the door opened, admitting an armed guard.

"You, girl. Get up and come with me."

Echo rose to her feet. "Where are you taking us?"

"Shut it and do as you're told." The man waved his weapon in the direction he wanted her to go. "Just you, not him."

"What about me?" David shouted as the door slammed.

"I'll deal with you when I'm ready," the jailer yelled. "You're destined for the mine, you are." Without a further word, he shoved Echo in the small of her back, forcing her to stumble along the corridor. Seconds later, they stopped by another door.

"Inside," he ordered. She pushed the door open and stepped through, spotting a familiar figure seated behind a desk.

"Marc!"

"Come in, Echo," he said. "Close the door behind you."

Echo did as directed and rushed over to him. Holding up a hand to stop her, he motioned to a seat, remaining silent.

"I thought you were dead," she said. "I'm so glad you're..." She paused and studied his face. This was not the Marc Pace she knew.

Something was wrong, his countenance unnatural considering the circumstances. The man behind the desk was relaxed and composed, having made no effort to rise as she entered. His face showed the same cool composure as always, without the slightest trace of stress. Echo sat back and raised her chin. "So, what's going on here?"

"What do you mean?"

"You're not behaving like you are a prisoner. You're relaxed, calm. What happened to the bad guys, the pirates?"

"Oh, they're still here. Take my word for it."

"Where are the crew and the other passengers?"

"They're being cared for."

The truth hit Echo like a sledgehammer. This man was not a captive of the bandits at all. Marc was one of them.

"Perhaps it might help if I told you where you are," he said. "This planet is *Kerac 5*. You won't find it on general star charts. It's what you might call a 'lost colony' or 'dark world', although 'off grid' would be more correct now."

"How … how are you involved?" Her lip trembled. How could he do this? He was so kind.

"Simple, Gorgeous. My family runs the place. This world and everyone on it belong to us." Echo sat dumbstruck, unable to find a response to the statement.

"Perhaps I should explain," he continued. "This planet was settled three centuries ago, before the *Barian* uprising. About a hundred years later, the only wormhole leading into this system vanished, cutting us off from the rest of humanity. What with one war or another, the colony was left off the newer star maps and vanished from the official records.

"Cut off from the galaxy and in danger of extinction, we survived, evolving from a simple mining concern—much like your own on *Corros,* I imagine—to a more stable agrarian society. We built farms, developed other essential industries, and lived tolerably well. The population is currently around twenty thousand people, although we did get as high as thirty-five."

"What happened to the other fifteen?"

"Not important. Twenty years ago, a new wormhole opened, and we found ourselves faced with a choice: to re-join the Federation that forgot us or to stay independent of the morass. We chose the latter."

Echo studied his face, her eyes fixed on his. "You said you own this planet?"

"Indeed, yes. My ancestor was the commander of the local naval detachment and took charge when the colony found itself stranded. We were only three thousand then. The family rose to be the power in this community, and we now control everything here."

"But you're a war hero. What about your career, your award?"

"Ah, a planned deception, I fear. My father, now departed from us, the Gods keep him, understood if we were to avoid forced reabsorption, we needed to take certain measures. We kept our renewed presence secret and sought allies and markets for our resources among other non-federated planets. There are many of them, outer worlds who want to be independent rather than vassals to the Federation machine."

"But you're…"

"An officer? My father decided it might be worthwhile to place someone in Fleet. He sent his youngest son—that would be me—to join the academy using false papers, suspecting it would work to our advantage. Thanks to you, that has now happened."

"Me? I don't understand."

"The research you stole from the Tolleani. The most useful item in there was the weapon that brought down Ben Teague's ship. Any vessel fitted with it can disable any other in space. The *Galicia* carried a cargo of the devices under my charge, for fitting to military vessels in outlying areas. Those units are now the property of my family and will be installed on our ships."

Echo remembered what she had seen on the airfield when stepping down from the truck. "I still don't get it. A few old freighters can't protect you from the whole Terran fleet."

"On the contrary." Marc sat back and smiled. "You don't know much about wormholes, do you?"

Echo squirmed in her seat. "No, nothing at all."

He lifted an eyebrow. "Did you ever wonder why passengers sleep during a transition? The process of traveling through a wormhole is disturbing to the human body. There is considerable discomfort, some pain, and the mind becomes disoriented, remaining so for several minutes after the jump. Experienced crews get hardened to it over time, but the disorientation effect never goes away completely.

"When a warship passes through a gateway, its shields are activated in case an enemy is waiting at the other end. This protects the vessel long enough for the crew to recover. Your clever little engineers figured out how to target any circuit on a ship. They can close down not only engines, but also defenses and weapons control, even through a defense shield.

"The Federation will eventually discover our new wormhole and dispatch envoys to explore. If anyone comes through, we'll be waiting. We will disable their shields and knock them out before they can recover from the transition. Then we will convert the ships for our use. Each will become another vessel in our little navy."

"They'll send more."

"A wormhole is not a large affair; the gate is enormous, but only one ship can safely pass through the actual wormhole at a time. A hundred could come through that gate, and as long as the crews are disoriented, we can destroy every one. With not a single one returning, Fleet will assume the gateway opens into a star or something equally dangerous, and give up. It's happened before."

Echo slumped in her chair, tears welling in her eyes. *To think I liked this man.* "What about your award? What was that about?"

"Ah … all a sham, as I said. I destroyed a Tollean ship— that much is true—but nobody ever knew I was there to meet it."

"I don't understand."

"My family has explored every avenue available to ensure our independence, including discussion with the Tolleani. We wanted to arrange for a treaty with them, and for reasons of their own, they jumped at the prospect of a human world aligning with them against humanity. I should add that was not our intention: all we want is peaceful neutrality and to remain independent. They sent an emissary to discuss terms, and it was my job to negotiate with them.

"Over the years of my service, I had gathered a crew of my own people, others from here who entered Fleet as I did, for our own reasons. We docked with the alien ship, but when two destroyers arrived unannounced, those stupid aliens assumed we had betrayed them and opened fire on us. I shot back."

"Did you honestly think any Tollean would deal with humans?" Echo already knew the answer.

"Unlikely, I agree, but if it all went pear-shaped, we knew we could keep them out as easily as the Federation."

"So you're a traitor."

"I don't see it that way at all. Everything I do, I do for the people of this planet."

"No, you do it for your own benefit, for your family."

Marc sat back and sighed, clearly irritated by her persistent defiance. "You know, considering your position, I hoped you would be a little more agreeable."

"Why? You'll only kill me."

"Not at all. I would like you to join me."

"What?" Echo could not believe she had heard him correctly.

"You and I share something. We attracted each other the moment we met—you can't deny that—and I thought you might find being my partner an attractive proposition."

Sparks flashed in front of Echo's eyes. She did not easily get angry, thanks to years of practiced patience alone on *Corros*, but Marc's words were downright offensive. "You arrogant—you've got to be joking."

"On this planet, Echo, I can be as arrogant as I like. I can offer you a life of luxury and all the power you wish, as a member of the ruling family on this world. You would never want for anything."

"I would not join you if you were the last man alive, you bastard. You disgust me."

"That's not true, is it? You let me screw you, after all." A smirk of satisfaction crept across Marc's face.

"I had an itch that needed scratching," Echo blurted.

The man's smile faded. "Perhaps a little time to think about it, then. Face the truth, Echo. You have no cause for loyalty to a regime that abandoned you for years on a distant world, and you could live well here. A few days might convince you that the best choice is to become my partner."

"Or die, I suppose."

"Oh no. We do not kill people here without good reason."

"Where are the passengers and crew from the liner?"

"They are alive and being looked after. I give you my word."

"What about Ben? The destroyer out there is his."

"Ah, my brother's new toy. The ship is useful, but my sibling is not as forgiving as I am. Your boyfriend is dead."

\* \* \*

Echo picked herself up and glanced around her new prison. After the confrontation with Marc and her extended and verbal response to his wonderful offer, the guards had marched her from the building and across a dirt courtyard to a smaller, one-story, concrete blockhouse, throwing her into the room in which she now found herself. An imposing and solid steel door blocked the only exit.

The room was about five meters square with a single, barred window overlooking the roadway. It contained little furniture, bar a small table and a mattress on the floor with a blanket lying in a tangle on top. At one end of the room, another door, wooden this time, led to what Echo hoped was a bathroom.

Once again, she was trapped, but at least this room was bigger. She ran to the window and looked out. The complex, as much as was visible, resembled the one she grew up in, but larger: this place was enormous, far bigger than the one her father had operated.

The wooden door opened with a bang, and a woman emerged from the bathroom. She looked to be in her early twenties or perhaps late teens, and a little shorter than Echo. Naked and unashamed, she stood in the doorway, wrapping a towel around her wet blonde hair. A smile spread across her face as she spotted the new arrival.

"Hi, sweetie," she greeted. "I heard the door; thought they'd come for the empties." She waved a hand towards a meal tray sitting on the table.

Echo eyed the tray; it had been hours since she had eaten, weeks if allowing for time spent in the stasis chamber.

"Who are you?"

"I should ask you that question. This is my cell, after all." The grin widened, revealing white, well-cared-for teeth. "Name's Diana."

"I'm Echo. I came down from a ship the pirates destroyed."

"Please to meet you, prisoner Echo." Diana ambled across to the mattress and retrieved a pair of cotton overalls from under the blanket. "You alone?"

"Yes … no. An officer came here with me, a man. I don't know where he is now."

"Oh, yeah, him. He's in the next room. The door in there slammed about half an hour ago, and someone has been doing a lot of yelling since. That'll be your boyfriend."

"No, not boyfriend. Just a friend."

"Oh, single?" Diana wiggling her hips. "Is he handsome?"

Echo tried not to laugh. This girl was as much a prisoner as herself, but still had sex on her mind. She had gray, laughing eyes and a bubbly manner despite being locked in this room. Something about her appealed, and Echo sensed immediately that this girl was a friend and possibly an ally. "Won't be much use to you in here, will he? And yes, he is cute."

"I don't plan to be here for long. My dad will rescue me."

"Sorry?"

"My father, the leader of the breakaways. As soon as he finds out I'm here, he'll come for me, again."

"Breakaways?"

"The rebels."

"Rebels? I don't understand. Isn't this whole planet a rebel world?"

"Oh, my poor baby," Diana said with a condescending smirk on her face. "You don't know anything about this place, do you? Guess I'll have to educate you."

For the next hour, Echo sat with her new companion and listened to the true story of *Kerac 5*.

Before the closure of the only path into the star system, the colony had operated like any peripheral mining world. When the planet became isolated from the rest of humanity, Marc's ancestor, the captain of the local naval base, organized the colonists to survive until contact with the outside could be re-established.

At first, it had been with the best of intentions, disseminating the people into farming and other activities to keep them alive in the absence of imported goods and services. Most of the mining operations closed, providing only what the population required.

Forty-three years ago, workers in the only still-functional mine discovered massive gold seams, and everything changed. Marc's father, assuming the Federation would return if the wormhole reappeared, decided the benefit of the find to this world would be minimal. The Pace family set themselves up as unopposed rulers, built an army of the worst thugs they could find, then mined and processed the gold using forced labour.

The massive mining complex around them was the result. Its underground workings were extensive, with kilometers of machine-dug tunnels. Local inhabitants provided the workforce, reduced to a level of virtual slavery.

*That explains the missing fifteen thousand,* Echo thought.

81

Unless employed in an essential activity such as food production, colonists ended up in the mine, resulting in the closure of schools and other services, and the almost total decimation of medical facilities. The Paces lived the life of royalty, showering favor on those who swore loyalty to their little enterprise. With virtually all weapons having been secured by the Pace army, the general population was powerless to resist.

When the wormhole reappeared twenty years ago, Pace formulated a plan to guarantee they remained hidden from Federation authorities. The ancient naval ships once used to protect the planet were refurbished and stationed by the new gateway, and any vessel stumbling through was destroyed or became an addition to the pirate fleet.

Contact was made with other unaligned worlds, and trade agreements were drawn. Despite this, the lot of the people stayed unchanged, all profits from the new regime flowing to the Pace family and its supporters. *Kerac 5* was now a slave world.

"Three of the family control everything now," Diana explained. "The old man died years ago. The oldest brother, Gordie, and the sister Janica, run the place. Then we have Marc, of course; real sleazeball."

Echo squirmed a little on the mattress. "Yeah, right." *I slept with him. Can't believe I did that.*

"So now they waylay ships out in space to build up their private navy and get more slaves. Somehow, they caught a new fleet destroyer, by pretending to be in distress, I expect, and it gives them enough power to take almost any other ship they want. Most of them are destroyed after the crews are sent to the mines."

"They use the crews as slaves?"

"Yes. Now that we have a new gateway, they're trying to move the local population back into other businesses, to make the colony more workable as a commercial entity. Captives from the ships replace them in the mine. There are hundreds of them down there. Most never come up again. Once in a while, one escapes and joins us."

Echo slumped back on the mattress, wondering if the passengers and crew of the liner were in the mine. She focused on the possibility that, with Ben's ship out on the airfield, he might be there as well, despite Marc having pronounced him dead.

"My dad's group stays in the badlands, inland from here," Dianne continued. "There are thirty-seven actives at last count, and our families. We live in the caves out there and do our best to irritate the collective Pace hide."

Echo let out a resigned sigh. "Oh Gods. What is it with mines and caves? That's all my life ever seems to be. How come you got captured?"

"Last night I snuck down to see a friend in the town. The guards saw me."

"What makes you think your father will rescue you?"

"Oh, yeah, I've been caught once before. The Paces don't have enough men to patrol everywhere. They have about five hundred men, but most of them are stationed in the towns along the coast and inland, to keep everyone in line. There are only about one hundred here at the mine, mainly because of the slaves.

"They don't see our group as a threat on account of we have no decent weapons, so the security is not that impenetrable. Most of the guards stay around the mine and the gold, and everything else is more or less ignored. They treat us as a nuisance and don't bother too much. Dad must know where I am by now, and he'll sneak in for me. You too, if you like."

Echo stared at her in dismay. *If I like?* Diana appeared to be an intelligent girl, but a little naive, as she had been two years ago.

"Deal," she said. "Tell me as much as you can about this place."

"Tell me about you first," Diana countered. "Like, who are you?"

For hours, the two girls talked. Night fell, and with no lamps, the room became dark. Diana climbed out of her clothes, lay down, and shuffled across to one side to make space.

"One mattress and only one blanket," she said. "We will have to share." Without a word further, she pulled the cover over herself.

For a few minutes, Echo remained motionless. She had not shared a bed with another female since childhood. Unsure how to react, she decided it was harmless. Easing down on the mattress, she lay facing away from her new friend, who seconds later rolled in behind and threw part of the cover over her.

"Gets colder towards morning," Diana murmured, and went quiet.

Echo lost track of how long she lay there. Having this girl's arm about her was strange. She closed her eyes and tried to suspend her sense of discomfort. A gentle snore came from behind her. Some hours later, Echo woke to find Diana's hand had worked its way under her singlet and now rested on her stomach. The girl was still asleep.

Beyond the window, it was still dark, but something had woken Echo. Outside the door to the room, someone was moving. Muffled voices came from the corridor, followed by a clank as the lock turned and the door swung inward. A bright light shone into the room.

# Chapter Eight

ECHO RAISED HERSELF ON one elbow as someone shone a lamp in her eyes from the doorway. A male voice whispered from the darkness behind the light.

"Di, you in there?"

"Yes, she's here," Echo said, nudging the inert figure beside her.

"What?" The blanket fell down as Diana sat up.

"Yep, that's you alright," the voice replied. Seconds later four young men stood inside the door, their lights now shining down to the floor. "Come on doll, time to go. Your Pop sent us."

Diana grabbed her overalls and dressed. "This is Echo. She's coming with us."

Echo jumped to her feet. "And David. He's in another room."

"I'm here," David's voice came from the corridor outside. "They found me first."

"We saw them bring the two of you in this afternoon," the man said. "Figured you must be important since you got the royal treatment."

*No*, Echo thought. *Just stupid. We would be down in the mine by now if that bastard Marc didn't want to make me his resident whore.*

The young man introduced himself. "Karl. Time's short, so let's go."

Without hesitation, Echo stepped through the doorway, straight into David's waiting arms. After hugging him, she turned to follow. Two guards lay unconscious on the floor in the foyer; the men did not give them a second glance as they filed from the building into the shadows of the complex.

In a dark, blind corner between two buildings, a heavy metal grate gave access into a drainage pipe. Echo's turn to climb in came just as a shout was heard between the nearby structures, accompanied by the brilliant flash of laser fire.

"In, now." Karl urged Diana towards the opening. Echo followed, clambering down rusty rungs until her feet splashed into water. For a few seconds she crouched, looking up at the laser flashes in the small circular window above. The light outlined the shape of others on the ladder. Rifle shots sounded somewhere above. Soon, the shouting ceased, and Karl dropped into the shaft, pulling the grate closed behind.

"It won't hold them long," he said, dropping the last few rungs. "Move. This place will be alive with more of Pace's men in a minute."

The passage out was an old, corroded steel culvert, running deep beneath the building complex and airstrip to divert run-off from the rains to a nearby gully. Karl shuffled along the pipe, the others following behind. He paused at a steel grill containing an open, steel-bar gate with a broken lock. No one spoke as the party exited the drain and made its way down the gully to the surrounding trees.

Like Echo's home world, this one possessed twin moons. Both were high in the night sky, spreading a warm half-glow across the countryside. The native forest was sparse, allowing the soft moonlight to filter down to the leaf-litter-covered floor.

Earlier, an anonymous hand had passed Echo a lamp, and now she and Diana led through semi-darkness on the way back to the breakaway camp. Not far behind, David followed deep in discussion with Karl, the other members of the team bringing up the rear.

"I'm going to be in deep shit when we get home," Diana mumbled.

"How so?" Echo asked.

"Karl and the boys had to kill those guards who saw us. We've never done that before, and Gordie Pace is going to be mad about it. Dad will be pissed with me."

*That isn't the half of it,* Echo thought. She wondered what Marc would do now.

Without warning, Diana stopped in her tracks, her hand reaching behind to stop Echo. "Don't move," she whispered.

Fifteen meters away, an enormous beast crouched on the leaf litter. Diana's light shone on the creature, its pelt so black it was like another dark shadow. Only the malevolent, pale, yellowish eyes betrayed its true nature. On the ground before it lay the ruin of some small forest denizen, the remains of a meal it had been eating when disturbed.

"What in the Gods' names is that?" Echo's heart pounded in her ears. "Is it dangerous?"

"They call it a *pantera*, and yes, it's deadly. Some type of cat from *Old Earth*, I think. This continent was mostly terraformed, so all the animals around here are from there, but this one is special. Gordie Pace keeps them as pets.

Sometimes he lets them out at night to hunt, and woe betides any locals who are in the way."

"Like us?"

"Yeah, like us."

The big feline rose to its feet, and with head lowered, crept forward, its eyes glowing in the reflected torchlight. A low, rumbling growl came from its throat as it pulled its lips back to reveal long, yellow fangs. Echo took an involuntary step back.

"Keep still," Diana hissed. "There will be others ... there." A second cat, larger than the first, stalked from the trees as she spoke and approached behind its mate. Both cats froze as several loud clicks came from behind the girls. Karl and the other men stepped forward, their rifles cocked and pointed at the threat.

For a moment lasting an eternity, animals and humans remained locked in a standoff until the beasts, first the smaller and then the larger, drew back, turned, and vanished into the night. Echo heard a collective sigh from her companions.

Diana slumped to the ground. "Holly shit. I've never been so close to those things before." She grasped Echo's leg and pulled herself closer. "You would not believe what they can do to a human being."

"Did you say they were pets?" David asked, stepping forward and squatting in front of the girl.

"Yeah. My Dad told me about them once. Pace has several. Apparently, one of the first mine supervisors started a private zoo back when we were still part of the Federation. Shipped all sorts of animals from *Old Earth* at his own expense. Various people kept it going over the centuries and kept breeding those things all this time. The Paces rescued this lot from there. He uses them like guard dogs."

"They obey him?"

"Yes. Somehow, he's able to control them. They keep going back to him, at least. He keeps them at the mine complex but lets them hunt in the forest, and sometimes in the shafts."

Echo drew in a sharp breath. "You mean they hunt the prisoners?"

Karl stepped up beside her. "So they say. Once he let them into a village near here, and five people dead in one night. I'll kill those things myself one day."

* * *

Day was dawning by the time the party left the forested area and moved into a drier grassland region. Towards midday, they passed through a small rural community, a typical colony settlement with dirt roads, water tanks, and worn timber houses. In a few open-fronted structures, small local businesses were opening for the day: a blacksmith, saddler, and carpenter. An old man in a leather apron looked up as the group drew abreast of his forge, raising his hand in greeting.

*Agricultural town,* Echo thought, walking in silence. *Farmers, or something similar.*

"This is one of dozens of communities up here on the plateau," Karl said as they walked through. "They grow food for the colony, raise livestock, and cut timber. These people help us with food and other things, and we try to protect them as best we can. Our base is in the maze over yonder."

90

Kilometers away in the distance beyond the fields, Echo saw a wall of rock, worn and twisted into the most amazing shapes imaginable.

"It's limestone—used to be a reef millions of years ago when the sea level was higher or the land lower. This used to be a seabed, and this planet had its own native life before we arrived. Water erosion has turned it into a mess of tunnels and canyons. Biggest on the planet."

"You hide in there?"

"We do not hide." Karl's eyes narrowed. "The Paces know we are here, but finding anyone in the maze is next to impossible without some idea where to search. It's also impregnable. I doubt if Pace can be bothered with us."

"He will be now. You broke into his compound and killed his men."

Karl looked at her, his face a frown. "Maybe not. He doesn't come after us as a rule and doesn't care about his men. I don't think he has enough of them to chase us and keep everyone in line as well."

"What about the townspeople? Why doesn't he force your location from them?" David asked.

"Tried once, but the villagers don't know our exact whereabouts. Every time he hurts a village, we go and wreck something of his, so now he takes the view that if he leaves us alone, we won't annoy him. That's what we are to him: an annoyance. That's how it's always been."

*Not any more,* Echo thought. *You stole Marc's prize whore last night.* "I thought you called yourself rebels," she snapped without thinking.

Karl stopped and gazed at her, a look of pity in his eyes. "We put lives first. You don't know what goes on here or how many men we've lost in the last few years."

Echo sighed. "Sorry. You're right, of course."

From the village, the group followed a rocky creek bed to the wall of the maze, then into a canyon, walking in the water to leave no discernible trail. The path was little more than a water-worn crack in the rock, many times deeper than it was wide.

Echo looked up at the horizontal striations covering the walls, the remains of alien, polyp-like creatures from long ago. Here, where the sun never penetrated, it was much cooler; after a while, she began to shiver, ill-prepared in the singlet and shorts she had been wearing since the moment David woke her on the ship. Hunger pangs pounded ever stronger in her stomach as she walked.

The narrow passage divided again and again. The path led up steep rock slopes and through passages and tunnels for hours, until the twists and turns merged into a total haze in Echo's mind. Lost, she was more than happy to accept Karl's statement it was impossible to find anyone in here.

Without warning, the final turn broadened to a wider, open space. A vertical wall rose for over thirty meters, overhung at the top to hide the bottom from the air. Echo stopped and gasped, taking in the unbelievable sight.

Opposite the exit point from the maze of canyons, a single entrance led into what looked to be a substantial underground habitat. Windows and shelves, carved from the solid rock, speckled the cliff face. In a few of these were faces, individuals seated in the openings carrying out a variety of domestic activities.

"None of this is visible from above," Karl said, stepping beside Echo. "The only way in is through the canyons, and nobody can reach us without substantial losses. We have several hideouts in here, and we move about."

"Please don't misunderstand me," Echo said, looking at the dark-eyed young man, "but is hiding all you do? Sit here and hit out when you can? Don't you have an organized plan?"

"Well, yes and no. What we don't have is guns. Pace would kill us if we became too much of a problem for him. Most of us are farmers who ended up here when the Paces took over our properties. We aren't trained, and what few weapons we have are old and ineffective against the Pace arsenal. That is about to change, I hope."

"How?" Echo stepped up to the entrance. Inside, hidden in the shadows, she saw two guards standing with guns pointed out of the opening.

"A new guy is helping us." Karl walked further into the coolness of the tunnels. "Months ago, Pace captured a warship, and now he uses it to pirate all the systems surrounding us. One of the crew escaped from the mines a while back, and we picked him up. We'll help him retake the ship and use it to strike back."

Echo's heart skipped a beat. *A crewmember.* He could tell her what happened. If one of them was alive, it was possible Ben and the others were as well. For the first time since seeing the destroyer in space, a real surge of hope rose in her breast.

The tunnel opened into a vast chamber, deep and broad, the ceiling supported by stone pillars left behind when the builders carved the rock away. She had seen something like this before on the few occasions she had accompanied her father into the shafts on *Corros*. The technique was typical of workings in shallow seams. This place was deliberately excavated to house a substantial community, but the principles were the same.

Around the edges of the main room, smaller tunnels and doors, some with curtains closing them off, led away to places dark and unseen. Numerous oil lamps lit the area, the floor scattered with tables, chairs, and workbenches. In one far corner was what appeared to be a kitchen with clay ovens set against the wall.

Echo watched an old woman open an oven and poke around inside. "Doesn't the smoke give you away?"

"We only cook after dark," Diana explained. "The exhaust feeds through pipes out into the canyons, well away from us to minimize risk, and we diffuse it as we release it."

"Sounds good," Echo said. *Been there, done that.* "How in the Gods' names did this place get here?"

"Hundreds of years ago, when they first terraformed the planet, a bunch of people came here from some place on Earth called Turkey, and cut these habitats into the cliffs. At first, they lived near the outer edges and farmed the surrounding flatlands, but after the wormhole vanished and the Paces took over, they moved further back into the maze, to here, and eventually disappeared. A lot of them went to the next continent, we think, but these places were empty, so we put them to good use. There are dozens of them through these canyons, but this is one of the largest."

Almost all the people in the cavern were female, women of all ages with a few small children scattered amongst them. They acknowledged the group as it entered, then returned to a varied assortment of activities. As Echo stopped and looked around, she saw in each of them the haunted, tired aspect of animals hunted their entire lives.

These were not rebels. They were refugees.

"Where are all the men?"

"Out on reconnoiter," Karl said. "They're preparing to snatch the warship. Should be back any minute, so you can meet the boss."

"The ship. Yes. What did you say the crew member's name was?"

"I didn't. His name is ..."

A noise came from behind them. Echo turned as a small band of men walked from the entrance tunnel. Several turned into side openings, but one stepped straight up to a table and slumped onto a seat, lowering his head with a loud sigh. Echo's heart jumped into her mouth, her head spinning. The face was familiar, those blue eyes and fair hair etched into her memory.

"Ben!" she screamed. "It's me, Echo."

# Chapter Nine

ECHO CHARGED ACROSS THE cavern and launched herself at the man she had thought lost and gone forever. Ben rose to his feet, bewilderment in his eyes as she threw herself into his arms.

"They told me you died," she cried, burying her head in his chest. "I thought I'd lost you." A second later, she pushed back and fixed her eyes on him. "What happened? How did you get here?"

Ben stepped forward and pulled her close again. "Echo. What in the Gods' names are you doing here?"

Tears welled as she realized she was once again in the arms of the only man she ever really cared for. "You first."

"They captured my destroyer. The bastards tricked us and boarded before we knew it was happening. We've been captives here since. These guys,"—he motioned towards the men watching the reunion—"found me wandering in the forest when I escaped. My crew are still prisoners in the mine."

"They got my ship too," Echo replied. "I was on my way to the fleet academy, and they stopped us at a gateway with your ship. I suppose the passengers and crew are being held in the mine as well."

Ben smoothed her disheveled hair with his hands. "The academy ... wow! How'd you escape?"

"I got off the liner before they could catch me, thanks to David." She pointed to the young man standing a few meters away, his eyes wide with shock. Ben's appearance, she realized, was not welcome to him, smitten as he was.

Diana also noticed his expression. She glanced at Echo and Ben, then moved up to put an arm around David's waist, smiling as he returned her gaze in mild disbelief.

*They would make a terrific couple,* Echo decided, hugging her own man tighter.

"The liner—your ship? The one I saw burning yesterday?"

"Yes. David got me down in a little bubble thingy, an emergency pod. We landed up the coast, but then they caught us anyway."

"Tracked you coming down, I expect. Pace has a pretty sophisticated setup, considering." Ben turned to the younger man and nodded his gratitude. David remained mute, Diana now standing hard against him and holding him close.

"Let's find a place to talk," Ben said. "This won't do. Somewhere private…"

"My room," Diana offered. "You're welcome to use it."

"Thanks, Di." Ben took Echo by the hand and led her into a side tunnel. A few meters in, he turned aside and parted a canvas curtain, leading her into a smaller chamber. The room was virtually empty; a pair of mattresses and numerous blankets and cushions lay strewn about the otherwise bare space.

"This'll do," he said. "We can talk here. You can't imagine how much I missed you." Without a second's hesitation, he pulled her close and kissed her, holding contact for so long she was sure she would suffocate.

"They caught us with our guard down," Ben said. "The bastards asked for help, pretended they had a disabled engine, and an injured crewman. When my away team went across to assist and look the ship over, they were forced at gunpoint to report everything in order and that they needed to bring the casualty back to the destroyer for emergency treatment.

"The four individuals crossing through the tunnel were supposed to be my medic, Miko, the other ship's captain, the injured man, and my engineer, but it turned out to be armed pirates, dressed in Miko's and Raj's suits. They overpowered my lock crew the second they came on board."

"Couldn't you stop them?"

"No. I was wary, but didn't realize they were attacking us until they stepped on the bridge and pointed guns at us. Stupid, totally stupid. Bad judgment on my part, enough to lose my commission."

"Why didn't your medical officer warn you?"

"She did, kind of. It made us wary, but we still didn't realize what was about to happen. They would have killed her and my engineer if she had been more obvious. I don't expect my crew to throw their lives away, and I don't blame her. If you get captured, you can always escape and retake the ship, but you can't get back a lost life."

"So what happened next?"

"Pace sent us down into the mine as slave labor. There's a maze of tunnels under that compound, and they keep over three hundred people there, forced to dig their bloody ore."

"Yes, Diana told me about it."

"Yeah. The mine's ancient, but a few decades ago, they cut into a new layer of igneous rock and hit the jackpot, vast quantities of gold in massive seams. Those Pace bastards are using it to create their little kingdom on this world."

"Gold's not worth much anymore, is it?"

"Well, no, and yes. Not as much as back in the days when it was the basis of most economies, but it still has enormous value in industry. It's a noble metal, used in almost every electronic device we have."

"How can the Paces trade gold with the Federation if they want to hide from it?"

"A lot of planets are not part of our union, and these guys are trading with them. The gold ends up in circulation through those worlds, and they protect their sources. Pace is using it to buy warships, I think. The plan is to build a joint force with the non-federation planets, with his family in charge. He calls it a home defense measure, but he's not fooling anyone."

"How can he get enough ships to beat the Federation?"

"He can't, but backed by the unaligned worlds, he can create one sufficient to make us leave him alone. Lucky for us, he's having them built new somewhere on an allied planet, and the first ships haven't arrived yet. The war against the Tolleani is enough for us to worry about now, so we won't push the issue. Pace can make his little empire without too much bother at all."

"How do you know this?"

A smile spread across his face, a low chuckle escaping from his lips. "One thing you can say about Gordon Pace: he loves to talk. Can't keep his mouth shut."

Echo sighed. "How did you escape?"

"Long story. I managed to sneak away during a shift change a few weeks ago. Wandered around for days before finding a way to the surface through an old exploratory shaft. Damn near didn't make it."

"Did they come looking for you?"

"No. Pace doesn't bother himself with little annoyances like an escaped prisoner. He uses his bloody cats—he calls them *pantera* or something like that—and lets them loose in the mines. Anyone caught outside the closed-off working area dies. Alex tells me only four have ever gotten out, including me. I gather Pace was away at the time, and I was out of the mine before he found out about my escape."

"Alex?"

"Di's dad. He runs this show."

Echo nodded, staring down at her feet. "I've met those cats. We ran into them in the forest on the way here. Are they really so dangerous?"

"Gods, yes. They're trained killers. Pace controls them through electronic implants: keeps a little device in his pocket that lets him give them a jolt of pain if they don't obey him. Anyone else who gets in the way is dead meat. How did you get past them?"

"We were too many for them, and I suspect they just ate. They weren't hunting. They came at us, but when Karl and his men moved up behind, they backed off. The Pace fam…"

"Yeah, they're a fine lot. Two brothers and a sister, the mother—the guys here call the old girl Ma Beagle; I don't know why—and a variety of relatives. They've set themselves up as royalty on this planet, ruling by force with Gordie boy as the king."

"And Marc as Prince Charming?"

"You know that arsehole?"

*I know him far too well*, Echo thought. "Yes. He was on the ship with me when it was captured. We had a shipment of the disabling devices, and he was supposed to be protecting them. You know he's a decorated Fleet officer?"

"Yeah, I heard they slated him for an award before I left *Cymbel 3*, but it wasn't until I talked to Alex that I put it all together. Traitorous bastard."

"He's also a fraud. The thing at *Borodino* was a fake. He went to meet the Tolleani, not to fight them."

"Where did you find that out?"

"He told me himself, before these guys rescued us from the cells at the mine compound. He's a traitor; tried to make me an offer I couldn't refuse."

Ben pulled her closer, fire burning in his eyes. "He didn't touch you, did he? I'll kill him myself if he so much as laid a finger on you."

Echo's heart missed a beat. How was she going to tell him she slept with the enemy? Perhaps for now at least, it was better to say nothing. "I'm fine. They still have your destroyer. They used it to capture the liner I was traveling on."

"Yeah, I heard. We plan to do something about that real soon. I intend to get my boat back. We were scoping out the airfield for a raid when you got here."

"Sounds familiar." Echo reflected on when she first met him on *Corros*. He lost his ship then and had been fanatical about getting it back. Nothing had changed. Vessel, duty, still and always first.

Tears welled in her eyes: in the last few hours, she had gone from joy at finding Ben to hating him for leaving her behind, to forgiveness, hope, and love. Together, they had survived a great deal on her home world, and now it was all happening again. "Haven't we done all this before?"

Ben looked down at her face. "I suppose so, but that was the Tolleani, and we only had to worry about ourselves. There's a lot more at stake this time. Besides the ship and my crew, there are several hundred slaves down in those mines and a whole colony under subjugation. We need to stop these guys."

"Before they and their allies turn on the Federation."

"No, that's never going to happen. We have hundreds of member planets, and a handful of sparsely populated worlds with a few dozen ships will never pose a serious threat. But they can run a terrorist operation for a long time, and we don't need a distraction like that while we're at war.

"How come the locals do nothing about it?"

"They do, or at least they try, but they don't have any weapons. The pirates collected everything years ago. Alex and his men have some old projectile rifles and such, but only a dozen able-bodied men. The rest of the people here are children, elderly, or women, and this planet has a culture where females aren't allowed to fight."

"But..."

Ben held his hand up to stop Echo's instinctive objection. "It's not a sexist thing," he said. "Most fledgling colonies try to keep any woman of childbearing age away from danger for obvious reasons, and it becomes ingrained in the culture after a while. The women here would not dream of fighting, except maybe Di. Kallister does the best he can."

Again, Echo sighed, wondering what she had walked into. "So, how will getting your ship back defeat Pace?"

"We can use it to disable his other ships," he said, "then go for help, return with the fleet, remove this regime, and bring the colony back into the Federation."

"What if they don't want to rejoin the Federation?

Ben peered intently at her. "They do. Pace doesn't."

Later, Echo sat alone in Diana's room. The habitat here was a maze of rooms and tunnels dug out by the long-gone group of colonists she had learned of earlier. The floor was gritty underfoot, the fine, irritating grains getting into everything.

Diana entered the room. "You two can stay in here if you like. Plenty of space."

"Won't that be a problem?" Echo asked. "With privacy?"

The other girl let out a little giggle. "No such thing around here, sweetness. People walk in and out as they please, since there are no real doors. If you see something you shouldn't, you ignore it."

"I'm not sure I like that."

"You'll adjust. We have heaps of vacant rooms, but most are further back in the complex. You want I should find one for you?"

In the evening—Echo knew the day had ended despite the lack of natural light in the refuge, by the fact the cooking fires were lit—she and Ben moved into their new room, a smaller, bare chamber along the same tunnel as Diana's. This one also featured an insubstantial hessian drape over the door, secured to pegs set into the rock above the opening.

Ben dragged his bedding, an old, straw-filled affair, into the new space and found some spare lamps, a water jug, and a basin. Echo preferred the privacy, the only real downside being that the toilet—a makeshift platform over a bottomless shaft in the rock—was minutes walk away.

Sitting on the mattress, she wondered how long she would have to stay in this hole. She had hoped this sort of thing was long behind her.

She was wrong.

\* \* \*

Two days later, she woke from her best night's sleep since arriving on the planet. Ben was absent, so she rose and headed down the corridor towards the main complex, assuming he would be in the common area.

At the entrance to Diana's alcove, she paused, planning to ask her friend if she had seen him. She reached for the hessian door drape, pulled the curtain aside, and looked in.

She froze and then dropped the curtain back into place. Di was not alone. Two naked bodies lay entwined in the corner of the room.

*Diana and David!*

She had half expected them to find each other in time, but busting in on them so soon was unexpected.

Well, she thought. Why not? She's smart and pretty, and he's ideal for her. Curious, Echo eased the canvas back again.

"You can come in if you like," Diana's voice beckoned.

Echo choked. "No, I don't want to interrupt."

"Oh, for the Gods' sake, come in."

Echo pulled the drape aside and slipped inside. She struggled not to stare at David, but failed. Unsure what to do, he rolled on his stomach and pretended she was not there, his face flushed.

*Better Di than me*, Echo thought. *You and I could never work, but she's perfect for you.*

"So … are you going to join us?" Diana crooned. "Could be fun."

"Um… No, sorry, I didn't mean to intrude. Have you seen Ben? I…"

Lost for words, and doing her best not to appear awkward, she backed to the doorway, turned, and moved away along the passage.

"Don't fret, sweetness," Diana's voice called from behind her. "I warned you. No one worries about privacy around here."

A soft murmur came from David. "I do."

"Sorry," Echo yelled back over her shoulder.

"Can you tell them we'll be down for breakfast in ten minutes?" Diana said.

"Yes, of course." Echo walked away as fast as possible.

In the dining area, Ben was conversing with a group of others. She assumed they were discussing the planned raid and stepped over to the table intending to join in. The second she approached, the talk ceased and the men looked down at the floor. Ben rose to his feet and took her by the elbow, leading her away to another table.

Echo pulled her arm away. "I want to know what's going on. I'm going with you."

A deep baritone came from behind her. "No, you'll not be going."

Echo turned to the owner of the voice.

The man standing there was tall and stick-thin, with a short, clipped, gray beard and piercing blue eyes. Alex Kallister was Diana's father, the leader of the breakaway rebels and the enclave. Countless scars covered his weathered face; this man was a fighter. He walked slowly, his head held high as he approached across the room.

"Where Ben goes, I go," Echo said defiantly. "I can look after myself—ask him." She nodded towards Ben.

"I am in charge here, young lady, and I will decide who goes and who does not. Tonight's mission is critical to us, and I'll not be taking anyone unless I am familiar with their abilities. Certainly not a woman."

# Chapter Ten

ECHO'S REACTION TO THE older man's ultimatum was instinctive. "that's just bullshit. I don't care…"

Ben grabbed her arm again and turned her to face him.

"Sorry, Echo, but you must stay here, for now. These men do not let their women fight or go into danger. They consider them too valuable and protect them whenever they can. That includes you. I know you are as capable as anyone here of handling yourself, but these people have customs ingrained into the culture for generations. Nobody here would dream of going against the rules, and we have to respect that."

"Ben, there are more women here than men. They could double his fighting force."

"They have no weapons," Ben repeated. "Only a few old ones—knives, projectile rifles, and such—against lasers and grenade launchers Pace brought in from outside. Kallister walks a fine line here, and the risk of death is always high. He pecks away at the Paces as he can, but he knows that if he goes too far, Gordon Pace will gather his forces and do something about it. I can change that, and I need you to work with me on this."

For a moment, Echo clenched her jaw and tried to think of a suitable rebuttal, then slumped on a bench and said nothing.

"Alex is not a bad guy," Ben said, watching the rebel leader walk away. "He's super protective of his people, the women and children in particular. The reason so many of them are here is that he keeps them alive. We need to respect that as well." He smiled, then returned to the clutch of fellow conspirators at the far table and picked up where he left off.

Minutes later, Diana and a still flushed David entered the room, fetched food from the communal kitchens, and joined Echo at her table. Echo concentrated on her thoughts, trying not to meet her friends' eyes.

"Don't fret over it, sister," Di said, referring to their earlier encounter. "Didn't bother me or David … right, babe?"

The young officer remained silent, his head down with eyes glued to his bowl, his face flushed. It was clear his embarrassment was not so much from the intrusion as from being discovered by Echo in particular. Diana had no doubt pressed herself upon him; the girl was not afraid to go after what she wanted—that much was clear.

*It'll do David good*, Echo thought. *They make an ideal match, and besides, it'll help to ease the tension between him and Ben.*

"That's not what I'm annoyed about," she replied. "It's the attitude around here."

"Oh, yeah. You've been up against my dad, haven't you?"

"Yes. How do you put up with it?"

For a moment, Diana did not reply, her mind clearly ticking over as she stared back at Echo. Her face was blank, a 'what are you talking about' expression in her eyes. Then, as she spotted the men planning across the room, realization dawned.

"I ... I suppose I just grew up with it. It's not my dad, just how things work here. There aren't that many of us, and my dad protects us as well as he can."

"And you don't think you should be allowed to fight?"

"Um... I've never really thought about it. I suppose I do, but Dad would never allow it."

Echo decided to drop the subject. She knew Diana well enough to know the girl was not lacking in bravery and initiative, but she also understood the situation her new friend had just expressed. All colony worlds protected their women until they stabilized. *Corros* had been like that, and remained so to a degree up to the time of its destruction. This world was no different. Its unique circumstances had just extended the concept somewhat.

Later in the day, acting on advice that Ben's ship had returned from its latest foray, the team left for the airfield. Echo, Diana, and David remained in the common area of the refuge until late into the night, waiting. The attack would take place at night under the light of the planet's twin moons.

\* \* \*

Ben took a leaf from Echo's book, choosing to create a disturbance near the mine while the rebel group snuck in to recapture the ship. Outside the airstrip fence, the surrounding ground lay in darkness, the perimeter lights all oriented inward. He crouched in the bushes beside Alex Kallister.

In the past few weeks, he had developed a deep respect for the old man. Kallister cared deeply for his people, but his effectiveness was limited by the lack of weapons and the reality that the citizens of the colony were cowed by their oppression. For all his efforts, he lacked knowledge of the finer points of leading a fighting force, but he at least tried.

Meters ahead, two of the men crouched at the fence, clipping an opening in the chain wire. Any minute, Ben expected an explosion from the direction of the compound, half a kilometer distant. It was unlikely all the guards would leave, but hope remained. Even in the direst emergency, a proper space crew stayed with their ship, but these men were not professionals, so there was a chance some would respond.

With luck, the distraction would allow the rebel force to snatch the destroyer, and perhaps relieve a few pirates of their lasers. Consequent to Echo's escape, Pace would be out for blood, so the more weapons Kallister's men secured now, the better their chances would be if the raid turned bad.

Beyond the lights, Ben's ship perched like an angry bird in front of the giant hanger, ready for the next journey into space. An interior light shone from the main entry above a lowered companionway. *Good,* Ben thought. Not having to get the hatch open made the whole thing easier and quicker.

Kallister had a simple plan. A group of six men would cross the field to a position behind the building, with three remaining outside to cover them as they crossed the exposed ground.

The attack team would sneak in, take out any men near the ship, and then board. There would be more bandits inside, and Ben hoped his men were enough to cope; Gordon Pace took the ship from him with just four men, so there was hope. Above all, it was a matter of surprise. Once in command, he would pilot the ship while the others did their best to work the defenses.

Not far away, a loud explosion rocked the night. The guards spun to face the main compound as a colossal cloud loomed into the night sky. Ben doubted much damage had resulted—it was homemade black powder, the only explosive available.

With a tap on the shoulder from Kallister, he moved forward and climbed through the opening in the wire, followed by the rebels. A quick sprint took them to the side of the hangar.

Ben was unprepared for what happened next. A threatening snarl drifted across the field, and three large, black shapes glided from the shadows to the open ground. The menacing cats stopped as a squad of fifteen armed men emerged from a doorway, their lasers leveled.

"I would suggest you drop those antiques and raise your hands, gentlemen," a calm, cynical voice said from nearby. Gordon Pace stepped forward, a small object clutched in his fingers. "Perhaps you would prefer to negotiate with my little pets instead," he added, extending the handheld device.

The cats were seven meters away, crouching low to the ground with all eyes fixed on their master. Ben looked across to the boundary, detecting a flicker of movement as the rebels outside pulled back into the undergrowth.

Pace also noticed the withdrawal. With a firm wave of his hand, he motioned his pets to the hole in the wire. For a moment, they wavered, creeping not as directed but towards him. The creatures obviously resented their subservience to this man. They hated him, but as he raised the control unit, they hesitated, turned to the fence, and slunk through the opening.

As the animals slipped into the darkness, Ben turned his attention back to the bandit leader. *How in hell did you know our plans?* Almost as the thought entered his mind, another figure stepped from the hanger. *Athol Brander.* Nearby, the other rebels gasped, and a curse came from Kallister.

"Traitor," he growled.

Brander was one of their own, an escapee from the mines who had joined them several months earlier. Now it was clear he was a plant, a spy, no doubt reporting every move they made back to Gordon Pace. The fierce burning in the eyes of Ben's companions told him that, should they ever get hold of the man, he would be dead in seconds.

"So now what?" Kallister asked. "You going to shoot us, Gordie boy?"

"Oh no. That would be senseless, would it not, dear cousin?" Pace said. "Do you think I'm a monster? For now, you can stay in the cells down below until I decide what to do with you." With a wave of his hand, he invited them to move away toward the mine.

*Cousin?* Ben thought as he moved away with the others. *Kallister and Pace are cousins!*

\* \* \*

Early in the morning of the following day, a disturbance at the entrance to the refuge gave warning that something was amiss. As the dim dawn light filtered down from the cliff tops, two men, both injured, trudged from the shadows of the stone canyons. Once inside the refuge, they sat at a table while the women attempted to clean and wrap ugly wounds on their arms and legs. Echo approached one of them.

"What happened?" she asked. "Where's Ben?"

"Captured," the tired and distressed rebel responded. "It was a disaster. We was betrayed. Those bloody animals chased us, damn them."

"The pantera?"

"Yeah. They was inside the airstrip compound. Three of us stayed outside the fence, and when the attack happened, we snuck away. But them cats caught one of us after we ran, they did. We lost Arvid."

"Ben—is he alive?"

"Maybe, maybe not. All our guys got took. Be back in the shafts by now, most like."

Echo felt her face burn as her annoyance with these people mounted. "Damn you, is he alive?"

The man peered at her, his face drawn and weary from exertion. "Sorry, girl. I think he was caught, but I can't say for sure."

"Do you think they took our men back to the mines?"

"I reckon so. Didn't see or hear no shots, so maybe they was captured. There's a pen in the mine where prisoners are put. Be there, I suppose."

"Do you know where, on a map of the mine?"

"Yes, lass, I do. I escaped from that hole last year. Won't help though. Got no men left, and no weapons. We're done, I think."

*Not a chance.* Echo stood and looked around the room at the grief-stricken women. "You might be surprised."

For the rest of the day, she remained in the room she and Ben had made their own. She fought hard to hold herself together, her heartache made worse by an awareness that the past was repeating itself. The events from *Corros* were happening all over again.

On her home world, she rescued her man only to have him taken away again. Now she had lost him, found him, and lost him again. She wanted to do something, but needed a starting point. These people were so cowed that it seemed likely they would meekly accept the loss and go deeper into hiding, instead of looking for a way to deal with their dilemma.

Echo sat alone, fighting to overcome the anguish invading her mind. Driven by hunger, she went to the main chamber, finding it filled with strangers. Diana rushed up to her.

"The Paces attacked the village," she said. "The villagers had some warning, so most of them escaped beforehand— one of our people brought them here." As she spoke, Echo noticed a stranger standing to one side, deep in conversation with one of the men in the rebel group.

"I know him," she whispered. "He's one of the pirates. I saw him in the administration building at the mine compound when David and I were prisoners."

"No, he's one of us. Pace isn't the only one with spies. We planted him months ago to have someone on the inside. He's the one who told my father when I was caught, and he managed to send word about the attack on the villagers. Without him, these people would be dead. He saved their lives."

For the rest of the day, small groups sat around the room conversing. Echo tried to take an interest despite the general exclusion of the women. Only one group concerned her, one that included the spy from the Pace complex, the survivors of the failed attack, and several of the male villagers. Sitting down next to her friend, she tried not to let her anger show.

"I think it's time we got involved here," she said.

"No," Diana said. "They won't listen to you. You're a stranger, and most of the people here don't trust outsiders."

"Then it's time that changed," Echo shot back, the slightest hint of anger in her voice. "Your father is a prisoner. Don't you think you should do something to rescue him?"

"Ye ... yes, but ... I..." For a second, her friend had the same resigned expression on her face as the others, then the look in her eyes hardened, and the emptiness gave way to a look of determination."Yes, I do."

"Good, then let's get started. You need to go and talk to the other women."

In a corner of the room sat an old, white haired man Echo recognized from the village. She moved towards him. "You're the blacksmith from the town, right?"

"I am that, girl, and you're the outworlder these boys rescued from the mine compound a couple of days back."

"Yes. May I sit with you?" The old man nodded, waving her to the seat. She sat and drew from her pocket a sheet of paper on which she had earlier drawn a diagram. "Can you make one of these?"

The image showed the crossbow she had treasured so much, now lost somewhere on the bottom of the ocean in the remains of the crashed liner. The old man took the paper and studied it for a few minutes.

"This is a weapon, right? A spring bow, with a string and a stock, to shoot a short shaft. Iron?"

"Wood. They're called bolts, and they're hardened wood."

"Metal might be better, the tip at least ... more punch. I don't got no forge no more, so no, I can't make it."

Echo leaned back and let out a sigh. "Damn. I hoped you could. Can't you set up a workshop here?"

The old man gazed at her, and then at the surrounding common room. His eyebrows arched in comprehension, followed by a brief nod of his head. "Possible, yes, miss." He dropped his eyes back to the drawing. "This trigger mechanism?" he asked, pointing to the sketch. "Can you make a detailed drawing of it?"

"Yes, of course." Echo had maintained and repaired her old crossbow for years and knew in minute detail how every part of it worked.

"Well, I can rebuild my forge. The spring I can make without too much trouble. I can use old leaf springs, I reckon, or even ironwood. The stock though…" He searched for another face in the room and motioned for a younger man to join them.

"This is our town carpenter," he said as the man joined them. "Gar, can you make a stock like this, and shafts like that, from iron-wood?"

For a moment, the young man stared at the paper, then nodded. "Yeah, a crossbow. I seen one in a book once when I was a boy. Why do you want that? The thing's useless."

"It's a weapon, and it can be deadly," Echo said.

"No use against a gun."

"It is if the person with the gun doesn't know you are there. It doesn't make a noise, and doesn't flash like a laser. I guarantee it. I used one to kill some aliens once."

The carpenter glanced up, his face filled with disbelief, and then studied the drawing again. "What about the trigger mechanism? I can't make that."

"The lass can draw a diagram for us," the blacksmith said. "I can do it if I can get my tools. Something like it, at least. We can sneak back to the town and try to retrieve them. I doubt if Pace's men bothered to remove them from the ruins."

"Yeah, possible, I suppose. We might be able to make one."

"How about a dozen or more?" Echo asked.

The blacksmith looked up at her in surprise. "What are you up to, lass?"

"Can you do it?"

"Can't hurt to try. Nothing else to do."

Leaving the two tradesmen to their deliberations, Echo walked up to the small huddle of men in the corner of the common room.

"So," she spoke. "How do you intend to get our men back?"

"Leave that to us," one man said without lifting his head.

"I don't think so. You're doing nothing but talk as far as I can see."

The man stood and glared at her. "This is not your business. Go sit with the others and let us handle this."

"Bull dust," Echo replied. "I don't care about your antiquated 'ways'. This *is* my business, and you need help."

"What do you suggest we do?" The question came from another, older man.

"She has no…"

"Shut it, Kas. What have you got to say, missy?"

"We go into the mine, rescue our men, and finish the job they began, to steal the destroyer back. Either that or you people live in fear for the rest of your lives. Your choice."

"We've got no weapons, other than a few old rifles. They're no match for lasers."

"In a full, front-on battle, I agree, but there are other ways to fight. As far as weapons are concerned, I can help, as long as you're prepared to open your minds to new ideas—and maybe an old one."

117

The old man stood and gazed at Echo, then turned his attention to the group. "Ben told me about this girl," he said. "She survived for years alone on an enemy-occupied world, rescued him twice, and destroyed an alien base with an antiquated bow and a handful of mines. You might want to listen to what she has to say."

# Chapter Eleven

A FEW DAYS LATER, Gar the carpenter and Raul the blacksmith appeared at the entrance to Echo's room with an oiled cloth bundle. Entering the chamber, Raul unwrapped the item and handed it to her.

"Oh, Gods." Echo ran her eyes over the beautiful device. The bow gleamed in the lamp light, the spring made of polished steel from a source she could only imagine, and the trigger mechanism from brass. The stock was from deep, red timber, shaped and finished by the hand of a true artisan.

"Will this be good enough?" Raul asked, concerned that the result of their labors might not be up to her required standard.

"Magnificent," Echo looking up at the men. "Can you make more like this, but without the beautiful finish to save time?"

"Yes. If we can get others to help with the legwork and leave us to what we're good at, we can make them up in another week."

\* \* \*

"How do you expect us to win a battle with these?" His name was Kaska, the young man who had confronted her earlier, and while a little set in his ways and fast to find fault, he had turned out to be a reasonable man.

The need to allow females to fight had been difficult for him to accept, and at first, he rejected the idea. When a delegation of the younger women, led by Diana, announced they intended to go after their men with or without him, he conceded, having no choice but to make the necessary mental adjustment.

"I don't," Echo replied. "Crossbows are only useful if you use stealth. We can send a small group armed with bows into the mines through the old tunnels your people used to escape. When we find a guard, we drop him, take his weapons, and move on until we reach the prison. If we are careful, they won't hear us until it's too late."

"They knew we was coming last time."

"Yes, because they had a spy in our camp. That's not the case now."

Mattius, one of the two who escaped from the first attempt to retake the destroyer, swore he spotted Athol Brander during that raid. One of their own, the man was standing with Gordon Pace when Mattius ran for safety with the cats hot in pursuit. No members of the original diversion party had returned, presumably captured along with the attack group. The only possible conclusion was that Pace knew their movements—Brander had betrayed them all.

Decimated by the unsuccessful attack on the airstrip, the rebels had only six men still in fighting condition. Other than the two survivors from the disastrous raid, four were older men who had remained to guard the caverns on that fateful night. With them were a handful of younger men from the village.

Diana stepped forward with three young women, declaring themselves ready to fight. Echo believed, looking at the defiance in Diana's eyes, that no man present would dare contradict her. The girl intended to rescue her father, and that was an end to it. Her friend's change of heart made Echo feel proud.

David also announced his intention to join the group. "I've never fought anyone in my life," he said, "but I'm strong and fit, and where Diana and Echo go, I go too."

Echo smiled to herself. She expected him to follow her, but he now placed his new love first. That was good, she thought, but she suspected he had bitten off more than he could chew.

The total remaining rebel arsenal comprised five old projectile rifles. Guns of any kind were scarce; the small collection was old and worn with limited ammunition, but the pieces still worked after years of careful maintenance.

True to their word, Raul and Gar produced six more crossbows and a large selection of bolts made from hardwood, all as sharp as needles. The new weapons lacked the superb finish of the first, but they functioned well and served the purpose.

By the end of the third week, the rescue team was ready. Every able fighter could use a bow to hit an object of human size at any decent range. Regular updates from their man in the pirate camp kept them informed on the state of the prisoners, still in captivity deep within the mine. Pace had decided not to kill them, preferring to break them instead.

The rebel spy also provided an old map of the shafts stolen at enormous risk from the mining office. The underground complex was larger than Echo imagined, with tunnels running for many kilometers in all directions.

"This is the original mine, here." Kaska indicated the dense maze of passages and chambers close to the entrance shaft. "These long shafts was dug looking for new deposits. This one here,"—he pointed to a long tunnel extending east from the old mine to a second maze—"is where the gold veins was found, and where all the work is done now. The prison is in this large space, here." a grimy finger tapped on the chart. "Dozens of tunnels run through the whole place, so it'll be easy to move around without being seen."

"So, how do we get in?" Echo asked.

Kaska ran a hand over the map. The only remaining rebel with firsthand knowledge of the mines, he was now the unofficial leader of the troop. He placed a finger on another line trailing south, ending about two kilometers from the entrance.

"Here. This is an old exploration drift, abandoned when it broke out into a deep gorge at the edge of the plateau. The outer end is open. I come out through there when I escaped — got lost, and ended up following that shaft. Almost broke me neck getting out."

"So we can go that way?"

"Yeah, but we need ropes to get down a cliff face to the breach. Tunnel might be blocked now; we'll have to risk that."

"What about guards?"

"Our spy says there's fifteen men stationed in the mine, all armed. One of them is at the inner end of this tunnel … here … and another here at this other shaft. I think it also leads to a way out, but I don't know for sure."

"What about the rest?"

"Three at the main entrance, three at the prison. The others guard the workers, so they're over here, by the work sites."

Echo studied the chart. "What happens if the guards are needed up top?"

"They lock the slaves up—here and ... here—and some of the guards go up. Six always stay to watch the pens."

"Six. I like those odds. We need to create another distraction, I think."

Kaska wrinkled his brow, concentrating. "We could start a fire," he suggested. "Isn't that what you said you did before, with the aliens? We could sneak people in to torch the compound. Might draw a few guards out; might not either. There are at least twenty more men in the barracks outside."

"Do we have any explosives?" Echo asked. "Mines, or something like that?" In her raid on *Corros,* she had used them to great effect.

"No, sorry. No more powder; fire's the best we can do. We got a heap of lamp oil. Those old buildings in the mine compound will burn like bonfires with this stuff, and we can make bombs with it."

Slowly, carefully, the group worked out a plan. The likelihood of there being two spies in their camp was minimal. On the small chance of a second, Mattius and Kaska, the designated leader of the new diversionary group, kept their exact plans secret. They hoped any guards would be at the perimeter gates, or other more obvious ways in.

\* \* \*

Crouched in the bushes, David swept his eyes over the mine compound. The chain wire barrier around the yard stood less than fifteen meters away, beyond a gap once cleared of vegetation but now choked with low, secondary scrub.

The Paces relied on the belief that nothing and nobody on this planet posed any threat to them, and considered another attack through the fence so unlikely that not a single man guarded this section.

At first, David expected the barrier to be electrified, as would any such on the more civilized worlds, but the rebels assured him that was not the case here. There had never been any serious threat or challenge to Pace's power, and local security had never been a concern. The fence was the easiest way in as it had been for the first, disastrous assault on the space field. The chain wire was exposed at every point, but Pace did not have enough men to patrol the entire length.

At first, they intended to enter by the pipe used to rescue David, Diana and Echo, but it proved impractical. Whoever was in charge of security did not intend that, path to be available to the rebels again. The gate at the outer end of the sewer was now welded shut, and five meters further in, a newer steel grill now blocked the way. The bars could be cut, but the task would take hours, so Mattius vetoed the choice, moving to the backup plan.

He prayed the pirates would not expect another attack, at least not in the same part of the compound. The barrier extended for kilometers, and Pace had no option but to concentrate his men at the mine and the airfield on the assumption there was little in the way of strategic targets in the administration area.

The aim was to sneak inside and set fire to as many of the buildings as possible. Most of the occupied ones were concrete or brick, but scattered among them were many old storage sheds, garages, and warehouses built from timber, weathered and dried over years of neglect. It was a potential tinderbox, and the rebel force would use it to its advantage.

The group comprised nine individuals. With David and Mattius were three of the older rebels who had remained behind as guards during the first, unsuccessful raid. Two men from the village accompanied them, with three of the younger refuge women who proved themselves capable at the brief training sessions.

At first, David insisted on going with the assault team, but Kaska refused him. The young officer had zero familiarity with ground combat or conflict situations, having lived almost his entire life in space, so the de facto rebel leader would not take him into the mines.

Diana, with her youth spent dodging the Paces, and Echo with her experience on *Corros*, both joined the main party, which even now approached the old exploratory tunnel entrance. Incensed and more than a little embarrassed at his exclusion, David agreed to join the diversion group only after a long, heated exchange with Diana.

With a gap through the chain-wire almost complete, he crept to the barrier, keeping low in the brush. Each rebel carried bombs made from oil-filled bottles with rags stuffed into the open necks, and a mine lamp with a shielded flame.

Once inside, the plan was to divide into three groups and move in different directions as far into the complex as necessary. From the furthest point, they would light the oil bombs, targeting the oldest and most combustible structures as they ran back towards the opening in the chain wire.

With the first and biggest fires drawing the attention of the guards, the chances of the attackers getting back out of the compound were excellent. An hour's observation had revealed few personnel in this part of the compound—the expectation that most of them would be at the mine or the airfield proved correct.

David's trio included, besides himself, one of the older men and one woman. On the way down from the refuge, he talked with each and was comfortable they would have his back, as he would theirs. Once through the wire, he turned along the fence line, following his companions to a group of old warehouses at the side of the yard closest to the airstrip.

The grounds were dark and silent. From building to building, the trio moved through the gloom, stopping at a gigantic, ancient, barn-like structure, the rear doors of which stood wide open. David grasped the first of three bombs from his bag and placed it on the ground, his fellow attackers doing the same.

His attention focused on his wristwatch—one of three timepieces possessed by the diversion party—he held his hand up until the appointed moment for the coordinated attack arrived. As the last second ticked over, he dropped the hand and each of the three opened their lamp, lit their fuses and lifted the filled bottles.

"One ... two ... three ... throw," the young woman counted. In perfect unison, three flaming bottles flew through the door of the barn, shattered on the vehicles parked inside, and splashed oil-driven fire across the floor of the structure. Within seconds, the old walls and mounds of ancient, canvas-covered equipment erupted into flame. Nobody waited to see the outcome; the group was already on its way to the next target.

From the moment they left the gap in the fence to the time all groups returned spanned only nine minutes, and in their wake, fourteen of the old buildings now blazed.

Throughout the compound, the roar of flames shattered the night. It would not take long for the locals to react.

David and Mattius reached the safety of the trees, turning to count their companions. Seven others besides themselves made it out—not one man or woman lost or discovered. Without further hesitation, they moved away towards the airstrip, intending to observe from a distance. Mattius expected more guards to be there, and the number might increase with the discovery of the fires.

When the pirates awoke to the situation, one of two scenarios was most likely. Either they would rush to the fire, or the Paces would decide it was another diversion and send them to the mine head or the airfield, expecting an attack on one of those sites. With luck, Pace would not expect the real action to come from within the shafts.

The only ways into the tunnel maze were the personnel elevators, the long access-ramp tunnel used to move machinery, vehicles, and ore in and out of the workings, and the two old, collapsed openings in long-abandoned drifts. All were watched, but most guards would be at the two principal entrances.

The destroyer being the target of the first push by the rebels, a second attempt on the same ship was logical. Kaska hoped that if Pace decided an attack on the field was imminent, he would send more men there, drawing them away from the mine. If not, the diversion group would take action.

From secure positions in the trees outside the barrier, they intended to use their few serviceable rifles to fire on the tarmac and create the impression that an assault was underway. A handful of old projectile weapons would fool no one for long, but they would serve long enough.

By the time the group reached the fence by the hangars, fire leapt high above the administration compound. With many buildings ablaze, the entire complex appeared to be in flames, small figures visible running among the structures, swathed in clouds of black smoke and lit by the swirling firestorm.

"Looks like at least some of the mongrels went to the fire," Mattius whispered from the shadows nearby. David grunted and sat down on a handy rock, waiting.

# Chapter Twelve

IN THE EARLY HOURS of the night, the penetration team made its way to a point between the compound and the coast. The mine sat close to the edge of a plateau, and in the past, the old exploratory tunnel had broken through into a deep cleft where the high ground shelved away to the coastal plain in a steep escarpment.

Echo leaned forward and looked into the dark ravine. "So where is it?"

"Twenty meters down," Kaska replied. "Not visible from here, but right below us, believe me. The brush on the cliff face covers the entrance." The descent was not difficult, according to Kaska, the only one of the party who had been this way before. Nevertheless, the group needed climbing ropes to reach the opening.

Despite the moonlight, the side of the cleft lay in pitch darkness. Kaska went first, scrambling down the near-vertical drop, setting the rope for the others to follow. His team, like the diversion party, comprised nine individuals. Other than himself, Echo, and Diana, they had the five remaining men still capable of fighting, and one of the refuge women.

Seven of them carried crossbows, the rest knives and machetes. The old rifles were of little use in the close confines of the shafts; the first shot would alert everyone in the complex to their presence.

They led with the crossbows, intending to use them to take out the guards stationed in the old tunnel. By the time they reached the active workings, they hoped to have at least one or two of the laser weapons that every guard carried.

At the entrance to the drift, Echo lit her oil lamp and crawled through the hole in the rock. The central mine area was another two kilometers away, a long walk through darkness in the old, narrow tunnel.

The passage itself was two meters square and hand-dug, the walls scored with the gouging of hand-held tools. A dank, musty odor pervaded the shaft, the reek of droppings from small creatures that had gained access in the past. Echo covered her nose with one hand, but it helped little to block out the smell.

A hundred meters in lay the end of an old railway line built by the original miners to remove the rubble as work progressed. The old, rusted rails were still solid after decades of non-use. The sleepers were treacherous, most of them rotten or eaten away by insects.

Silently, the party crept forward, walking two abreast in the narrow space. In the lead, Kaska carried a mine lamp while beside him, Echo advanced with her crossbow armed and raised, ready to fire on anyone they might stumble across without warning.

After an hour of moving through the oppressive mine, Kaska motioned to turn down the lamps. "Not far now," he said. "This tunnel opens into a wider passage in the old complex—we can use it to reach the new workings and the prison."

He pulled out an old, battered timepiece and studied it for a moment. "The diversion should've begun twenty minutes ago. The fires should be in full swing now, and with luck, some of them guards in the mine have gone out to help."

With one lamp burning low for illumination, the group proceeded until a glow appeared ahead. The larger thoroughfare blazed with powerful arc lights, the glare filtering a short distance down the smaller tunnel. With the oil lamps doused, Kaska and Echo moved forward alone, keeping against the walls.

At the junction of the tunnels, the guard post sat in a corner bay carved from the solid rock; on advice from their spy in the Pace camp, Kaska expected to find only a single guard posted here, but voices filtering through the otherwise tomb-like silence said otherwise.

Only one of Pace's men was within sight, talking on a telephone. After several nods of the head, he hung up and turned to another man somewhere at the back of the alcove.

"Better get offer that bunk," he barked. "You're wanted upstairs. Something's going on up there."

"Yeah? What?

"How in the Hells should I know? Move, before the boss feeds us to his bleedin' cats."

The second guard stepped into view, muttering beneath his breath. He picked up a rifle from against the wall and shuffled away.

"Move, you bloody fool," the first man yelled after him. "Pace don't like being kept waiting."

The man's footsteps faded in the distance. Kaska crept forward until he could see the remaining guard, once again on the phone, reporting his companion was on the way.

131

Replacing the handset, the guard spotted the rebels standing only meters away. A bolt from Echo's crossbow dropped him to the floor, a look of alarm frozen on his face.

"Not bad with that thing, are you?" Kaska said, picking up the guard's laser pistol.

Echo retrieved her arrow from the corpse. "I've had a little practice."

Minutes later, she, Diana, and Kaska crouched behind a massive excavator, parked in the largest underground space Echo had ever seen. The primary machinery storage depot of the original ancient workings was hundreds of meters long, at least one hundred in width, and fifteen deep. Like the mines on her home world, colossal stone pillars left during the excavation of the vast chamber supported the ceiling.

At the far side of the cavern, a scaffold column marked the terminal where twin elevators carried personnel up through the ceiling into a shaft from the working level to the surface. To one side of the elevators, an arched entrance led to a sloping tunnel, the ramp whereby heavy machinery came and went, and the extracted rock and ore were removed. Two armed guards stood at the base of the elevator gantry.

"Apart from the old drifts," Kaska said, "them elevators and the ramp are the only ways out. They're always guarded, but if we can rescue our men and collect a few more weapons, we might escape that way. The lifts are out—the pirates will trap us in them. If we use the ramp, we can reach the top before they knows we're coming."

Diana crept up beside him. "So, where do we go from here?"

"We leave one man to keep an eye on these guards, and follow the service tunnels to the new workings. By now, the prisoners will be back in their pens. We break out our guys and the others. Any guard we see, we kill and take their weapons."

Creeping away from the excavator, they inched their way towards the rear of the chamber, then headed towards the newer workings, skirting the larger access-ways and following minor tunnels wherever possible.

Before long, they located the pens where the workers were kept when not being forced to dig at the gold seams. The cages were simple chambers dug into one side of a larger excavation, the entrances set with grills cemented into the floor and ceiling of each opening. As expected, Pace's men had locked the slaves in before going topside to help with the fires.

On the opposite side of the main chamber, several similar but smaller alcoves served as the prison. Echo crept forward and slipped behind a canvas-covered stack of crates, seeking a better view of the men sitting against the rough walls of one cell.

"Ben," she said under her breath, recognizing a dark shape she knew without doubt to be her man.

"Looks like they're all still alive," Kaska whispered as he and Diana joined her. Only a handful of armed men occupied the room, their attention on the prisoners and their backs to the entrance. "I guess our diversion worked this time. The other guards will be on their way to the compound or the airstrip."

"Only four," Echo said. "We can take them out together —one hit."

From behind the stacked equipment and stores, the members of the raid team picked their targets, and on Kaska's signal, fired with crossbows and the commandeered laser pistol. Seconds later, four bodies lay dead on the dusty rock floor, and a deathly silence filled the chamber for the briefest of moments.

Everyone shouted at once, slaves crying for release and the captured rebels calling from the cells. Echo grabbed a ring of old, iron keys from the belt of one body and rushed to the bars of the cell holding Ben.

"I figured you would turn up eventually," he said, grinning from behind the bars of the enclosure. "Let us out, quick."

"This is getting to be a habit, don't you think?" Echo rammed the key into the old lock and twisted hard. The second the door opened, Ben rushed out and grabbed her, pulled her close, and kissed her.

"I suppose so." He ran his hand through her hair and gazed into her eyes. "We need to stop doing this."

"Agreed," she said, looking at the men pushing past them into the main chamber. "But not today."

At the far side, the prisoners clamored for release from their cages. The pens were packed with haggard, desperate individuals of both sexes and all ages. Among them stood children no more than ten years of age, and several elderly men barely able to stand without help. The constant babble of frantic voices filled the cavern. Echo screwed her nose up at the overpowering odor.

"How did you find your way in here?" Ben asked as they moved across to where Kaska, Diana, and her father talked in a huddle. Alex Kallister glanced up as they approached, peering at Echo with curiosity and a new respect.

"Crossbows, for the Gods' sake," he said. "Brilliant, young lady."

Echo brushed the praise aside. "We have lasers now, from the guards."

"Yes, but not enough. There will be more of them up above, so we are still at a disadvantage." He turned his attention to Kaska. "I doubt if your plan to take the ramp will work."

"We can always leave the way we came in," Kaska suggested.

Kallister appeared to consider the idea for a moment and nodded his head. "It will take hours to move all these people along the drift tunnel and up the cliff, and Pace will be waiting for us at the gorge if he works it out."

"Are there many guards above?" Echo asked.

"Likely, yes. Your diversion should see most of them either fighting the fire or defending the airfield from your mock attack. A few of us can stay behind to keep the rest out of the mine while we take everyone out the back way. As long as they think we are still in here, they will likely not work out how we are escaping."

"I'm going out now, through the drift," Ben said. "How long from here to the air strip?"

Kaska stared at the floor for a moment. "A small group? An hour, maybe. No need to waste time sneaking about this time."

"Me, my crew, and you to show us the way?"

"And me," Echo added.

"Yeah," Ben replied, a smile creeping through the grim set of his face. "And you."

Kallister nodded. "What do you intend to do?"

"I plan to finish what we started. The minute the Paces wake up to the diversion, they will guess something is wrong here in the mines and send their men back to the pithead, so they will have minimal guards at the airstrip again. We have lasers now, so we take them out, get my destroyer back, and blast the compound. We finish this now."

"I'm not so sure it's a good idea. We tried it once."

"My destroyer is the only hope you have of defeating the pirates. I'm going, and my crew with me. This is your last chance."

The rebel leader nodded. "Fine. You get going while we organize the prisoners." He motioned assent to Kaska, turned, and walked towards his men.

"Is it so important to get the ship back right now?" Echo asked.

"Yes, more than ever now. If Alex gets them out through the back tunnel, they still have to fight Pace. He has a small army, and the rebels aren't strong enough even with the weapons from these mines. The only way to end this is with my boat. We immobilize Pace's fleet on the ground— my destroyer can level the entire airfield—and attack Pace from the air. Then we go for help."

Without another word, Ben waved Kaska on, he and his crew following into the tunnels leading to the old abandoned drift. With a sigh, Echo trudged after them.

As she strained to keep up, she realized the individual beside her was a young woman. Echo did not recall the girl's name, but remembered a meeting long ago at the commissioning ceremony for Ben's ship.

The woman had been different then, well-groomed and attired in dress uniform. Now she wore the ragged remains of a flight suit, covered in filth. Tired and worn, she and the other crewmembers walked with purpose, their hollow, sunken eyes blazing with faint flashes of fire. Freed from a hell Echo might only guess at, these people were out for blood.

# Chapter Thirteen

GORDON PACE JUMPED DOWN from the vehicle and stood beside his younger brother. The mining compound blazed, flame soaring meters above the roofs of the buildings. With news just received that robot drones had passed through the gateway and were attacking his patrol ships, a fire was the last thing he needed. It would not be long before Fleet ships followed the robots; time was short.

"What in all the Hells is going on," he bellowed, trying to make himself heard over the roar of the flames and the racket from the dozens of men fighting the inferno. Marc turned and motioned his older brother aside to a position where a concrete wall shielded them from the blasting heat.

"Started in the warehouses. Those buildings are as dry as old bones, and they burn like bonfires. The men are doing their best, but we're losing the battle. The fire is spreading to other structures in the complex."

Gordon peeked around the end of the wall. "How did this happen?"

"Nobody knows for sure. The fence down by the old drum stores has a hole cut in it, so I'm guessing it's the work of those rebel mongrels again. This is trying my patience."

Gordon leaned against the stonework and tried to fathom why the rebels would want to burn the compound.

"This has to be another bloody attempt at a diversion. How many men do we have watching the airfield?"

"Enough. I sent an extra dozen over—had the workers down below locked up and pulled the guards up to help here…"

A loud klaxon sounded from the direction of the mine, drowning him out. He noted the startled expression on his brother's face as they both realized the real reason for the diversion.

"Take as many as you can back to the shaft entrance. That's the target. They're trying to rescue our dear cousin."

Marc's attention wavered between the burning buildings and the distant siren. "What about the fire?"

"To the Hells with the fire. Let the damn place burn to the ground. Set the explosive charges in those two old tunnels off now so the only way out is by the front entrance, then shut the elevator cages down and put every available man outside the ramp tunnel. Kallister will have no choice but to come up that way."

A man ran towards them from the administration block, one of the few buildings yet untouched by the inferno. For a few seconds, he conferred with the older brother before heading off towards the airstrip. Gordon turned back to Marc.

"Send Harlow to deal with the situation at the mine. We have bigger problems."

"What's gone wrong now?"

"Ships have broken through the gateway and are on their way here. They'll arrive within an hour, and we need all ours up before they do."

A puzzled look appeared on Marc's face. "How did they avoid our blockade?"

"A swarm of unmanned drones came through first, and kept our boys engaged while manned warships came through behind. Only one of our ships survived long enough to send a warning. Four contacts are heading our way now: I'm guessing they're all warships."

"Robot drones? Damn, we didn't allow for that. How did they find us?"

"You're the spacer, brother," Gordon spat, turning and stalking towards the airfield. "You tell me."

"They have to be military—Federation," Marc said as he followed his older sibling. "The drones prove they knew what to expect, that we would be waiting on this side of the wormhole. We can't stop them with one destroyer and a bunch of armed freighters and antiques. We've only just started installing the disabling devices."

"That is not my major concern. Our escape from here is."

"You expected this?"

"Baby brother, your naivety amazes me sometimes. Why do you think I moved our gold off planet? We sneak away and hide in the outer reaches until things settle, then head through the gateway to one of the unaligned worlds. *Aceron*, I think."

"The family…"

"…can be ready in fifteen minutes. Call them in. I want them at the airstrip now."

\* \* \*

After their release from the pens, Alex Kallister and his men, armed with weapons removed from the guards' bodies, advanced down the passage connecting the new workings with the main depot.

In a side chamber of the thoroughfare, they found a guardroom. The door took only minutes to break open, and a dozen lasers and a box of power packs were added to the rebel armament. Kallister doubted they were enough, but it was better than what they had.

A loud klaxon sounded from ahead. "Well, I guess our secret is out," he said as Diana and several of the men led the freed prisoners into the side tunnels towards the drift entrance. "The rest of us will head for the depot. With any luck, we can reach the elevators before Pace's men can come back down, and we might stand a fighting chance."

The battle to take over the entrance complex proved far less difficult than Alex expected. With the other guards having gone to the surface when the alarm sounded, only two remained. They faced the elevator structure, drawn by the muffled sound of a siren at the surface, and expecting trouble from above, not from behind.

When the rebels entered, they turned, but had no time to raise weapons before they lay dead on the floor, riddled with laser fire. Alex posted guards at the lifts and turned his attention to the nearby exit tunnel.

The archway marked the start of a long, gentle slope that rose for almost half a kilometer before switching back on itself to come out not far from the pithead. The ramp was now the only avenue for anyone wanting to enter in force, or leave.

At that moment, the sound of thunder rumbled through the workings, followed soon after by a cloud of dust from an opening at the back of the cavern.

"Damn," Alex cursed. "They mined the exploration drifts. Diana is down there." Without hesitation, he motioned two men to follow and rushed in the direction of the explosions. Dust and debris choked the tunnels, making breathing almost impossible. With his shirt pulled up to cover his mouth, he forged on, almost colliding head-on with a mass of bodies rushing towards him through the darkness. "Diana, where are you?"

"Here—over here." A small, grime-covered figure emerged through the crowd and stumbled into his arms. "The old drift is gone. Must have been rigged for emergencies."

"Anyone hurt?"

"No, I don't think so. We only just reached the guard post when the blasts went off. None of us was inside."

"How far ahead of you was Kaska's group?"

"They should be safe. The explosion was near the inner end … with any luck, they were well past the blast zone."

Alex hugged his daughter closer and turned back towards the depot. His available options had narrowed to a single choice. With the old exploration tunnel collapsed, the ramp was the only escape route for his men and the rescued prisoners. Pace would be at the top, waiting.

\* \* \*

Barrett Harlow hunkered down beside his vehicle and squinted across the apron. Ahead, the gaping, floodlit mine entrance bored into the vertical wall of the old open-cut excavation. The access sloped down, allowing a clear view inside for a little more than thirty meters.

Remotely triggering the destruction of the back shafts had been Harlow's first action. The only ways up from the galleries were now the elevators or the tunnel; no one was coming out either way without his approval.

"So, what's the situation? Do we know?" He directed the question to a stocky guard beside him.

"Possibly, Sir. I'm guessing that ass Kallister is loose down there. Somehow, he and his men must've gotten out of the cages and overpowered the guards. The whole bleeding lot of them are probably free now, and armed."

"The rebels must have come in along the drifts after starting the fire and let them out. Are the security cameras still working?"

"Nah, they took them out after the alarm went off. Don't matter, though. We got em penned up."

"Don't be so sure." The mine below contained a great deal of equipment; Harlow knew the rebels could use any of a dozen machines to ram their way out, using the steel of the heavy vehicles as shields. "Come on. We've got work to do."

Thirty minutes later, dozens of massive dozers from an old open-cut section of the complex sat on the apron, parked in a semi-circle around the entrance with their blades facing in to form an impenetrable barrier. Between, under, and on the machines, over one hundred armed guards waited for what was to come. Harlow grinned as he surveyed his makeshift killing field. Nobody was coming out alive.

* * *

Echo scrambled over the rocks above the cleft and crawled into the bushes. The trip back along the drift had been unpleasant. Halfway between the guard station and the breakout in the escarpment, an earth-shattering rumble sounded somewhere behind them. Seconds later, a wall of dust blasted through the tunnel and enveloped them, making vision difficult even with the aid of the oil lamps and pilfered torches.

The choking debris clogged eyes, filled nostrils, and made breathing impossible, forcing the party to wrap cloth around their faces and feel their way along the unseen walls towards the exit. The last stage of the passage through the old shaft took twice as long as expected, until at last the group lay sprawled on the ground at the top of the cliff, wiping the grime from their skin and batting dusty filth from their clothing.

Echo gasped. "That was fun. What now?"

"Now we head for the airfield," Kaska said. "That explosion was deliberate, and I think I heard a siren before the bang. I reckon Pace set mines in the tunnel just in case."

Ben pushed himself back to his feet. "Might be good for us. If that was an alarm, the Paces have figured out what's going on. By blowing the old shafts, they have everyone cornered in the mine, so they'll send every guard they can spare to the shaft head to make sure nobody comes up that way."

"Not good for our guys," Kaska commented. "They're trapped."

"Even more reason for us to move. The best thing we can do for them is get to my ship. We can blast every square meter of the apron and clear the way for Alex and the others. Come on." Without a further word, Ben took Echo by the hand and headed through the undergrowth toward the airstrip.

A loud roar rose from ahead as they approached the field.

"Those are engines," Echo shouted over the noise as she rushed through the scrub. "They're taking off."

"Not my boat," Ben said. "I know the sound. Must be one of the other ships." The words had barely left his mouth when another roar joined the first, and another, filling the night with an ear-splitting cacophony.

The party rushed on, reaching the airfield at the place where Ben's original sortie passed through the fence. Out on the strip, several of the converted cargo vessels comprising the bulk of the Pace navy lifted into the air, sending clouds of dust swirling around the small groups of individuals boarding the remaining ships.

Forty meters away, Ben's destroyer crouched on the tarmac. A single worker struggled to disconnect a ground tug from the forward landing gear. The companion ramp was down, and lights shone from the open hatch.

"Here," a voice whispered. "Over here." David's face appeared ghostlike through the shadows from the cover of the nearby vegetation.

"What's happening?" Kaska asked as the group joined the diversion party.

"Hi, Echo," David greeted, ignoring the question. "Where's Diana?"

"David!"

"Oh, sorry—they started powering up the ships fifteen minutes ago. Some have lifted off, loaded with civilians. I think they are leaving. So, where is Diana?"

Ben crouched down beside the younger man. "What are they doing with my ship?"

"They just pulled it out onto the tarmac. There are two men aboard. Five more in the hangar, and one on the tug. They're going to take her up."

"Not on my watch." Ben turned to Kaska. "We don't have time to wait. We need to go now." Turning back to his crew, he raised his hand. The others reciprocated, raising borrowed weapons to show their readiness. Echo had passed on a laser weapon; she much preferred the crossbow made by the men at the refuge.

Ben leapt to his feet and advanced across to the fence, with Echo and the crew close behind. Kaska followed, leaving David and the less well-armed rebels outside as a backup. The hole in the chain wire made on the first attempt to take the ship was still unrepaired, and the cut-away piece was secured back in place with wire ties. A few solid thumps from Kaska's booted foot pushed it free again, and the group scrambled through the gap.

The tug driver lifted his head as Kaska ran across the tarmac. The shape of a man running towards him was the last thing he expected, and ever saw. Soon the crew crouched around the base of the ship's gangway.

"I don't want weapons fire on the control deck," Ben said. "Damage to the consoles could disable the ship."

"The boy said two men are on board," Jerry Bayer said. "How do you suggest we deal with them?"

"We sneak in and restrain them. With any luck, they will be so absorbed in the power-up procedures they won't realize we're here. Echo, you and Miko stay here and keep an eye on our backs. If anyone comes, yell." Without a sound, he crept up the gangway and into the cabin, followed by Kaska, Jerry, and the remaining crew.

Echo turned towards the hangar and crouched behind the steps. A little annoyed Ben had left her behind, she nevertheless understood his logic. In the close interior of the destroyer, her crossbow was useless. With lasers out of the equation, this was going to be a hand fight.

Miko Bay, Ben's medical officer, squatted behind her, looking in the opposite direction. "There goes another one," she said as a cargo vessel lifted and slid away over the mine compound. "The people boarding were civilians. I spotted women and children among them. Some of them were quite elderly."

"Let me guess. One of them was tall, thin, and looked like she should be dressed in an evening gown and a fake fur?"

"She was wearing a stole. You know her?"

"Oh yes," Echo thought back to her first meeting with the 'wolf lady' on the cruise liner. "Lady Amanda Britton, the Pace brothers' aunt. It would have been her."

"So why would they be loading their relatives on ships at a time like this?"

"Pity you will never have the chance to ask her yourself," a voice came from nearby.

Echo spun on her heels, her loaded crossbow raised and ready. A solitary figure stood silhouetted against the floodlights of the hangar. She did not need to see his face to know who it was.

"Marc." Hatred surged, flooding every corner of her brain as her mind flashed back to the time with him on the passenger ship. Here was the man who had charmed and seduced her with full knowledge of the attack to come, and then betrayed her.

"Sorry, Love, but no," the silhouette replied. "I suppose we are alike." He walked slowly, moving across until the light played on his face. He resembled Marc, but there was something different, older, and harder about him. "Name's Gordon ... but you know that now, don't you?"

Pace circled until reaching a spot between her and the opening in the fence. Echo prayed that David, or one of the rebels hidden in the trees, would take him down. They had only the old projectile weapons, but those could kill.

Pace's mouth twisted into a cynical smile. "You're that Bourke bitch my baby brother is so enamored with. Never could trust the boy to keep it in his pants."

Miko glanced at Echo, a puzzled expression in her eyes. Echo shook her head, keeping her eyes on Pace. He held a laser pistol, but it was the object in his other hand, a small black box, that drew her attention. She had talked many times about this man with Diana and the other rebels, and she guessed what the device was. A noise came from behind her.

A few meters away, three black shapes crouched on the ground beneath the destroyer, having crept up while Echo was focused on Gordon Pace. The big cats remained motionless, emitting low, threatening snarls but keeping position, their eyes fixed on their master.

Echo knew that look, the look of hatred. The creatures were under Pace's control, and when they did as directed, they were fine. When they disobeyed in any way, small implants beneath their skin delivered painful shocks to their nervous systems.

"My dear brother shows remarkable taste, I must admit," Pace said, "but I'm sorry to say he's left you. The ship that just left is carrying the majority of the family, including Marc. Once my men join me and we deal with your little band, I will follow them and head for safety. By the time your fleet gets here, we will be long gone."

"Fleet?"

"Oh yes, of course you wouldn't know, would you. A squadron of Federation ships is on its way. Be here any minute, I should think. All they will find is a bunch of fools I have positioned outside the mine. I will be around the far side of the planet and heading out into the system."

*David's distress drone*, Echo thought. *It was located and traced here*. Her distaste for this man swelled as she listened to him without taking her eyes off the cats. *Come on David, where are you?* "You'll never get away."

"Oh, I think we will," Pace replied. "It's impossible to guard a jump gate completely, and we can sit out in this system's Kuiper Belt for months if need be, waiting for our chance. Do my pets concern you?"

Echo did not respond, aware that she and Miko could not take down both man and cats in one hit. She would never have time to reload her crossbow, and the rest of Pace's men would be here soon; at least four more were in the hangar, according to David.

A loud bang sounded from beyond the fence. Gordon Pace ducked and half turned as Echo took aim with the bow and pulled the trigger. The bolt flew true, piercing her target in the wrist above the hand clutching the control box. Pace yelped as the device spilled from his grasp, then collapsed as Miko fired a laser blast at his legs.

The second he hit the ground, the cats reacted, and both women turned to face the new threat. The creatures crept forward, gliding across the asphalt, but not towards them. They moved instead toward the man who had tormented them for so many years.

The pirate leader had turned them into his personal assassins, but now Echo saw the fallacy of his methods. Born killers, the animals were used by Pace as such, using the implants under their skins to force them to obey. Rather than train by reward, he controlled with pain, and now he would pay for that approach. They were well aware that the source of their torment was the little black object always held in their master's hand. That was not now the case; their instinct to kill the man they hated took control.

"Quick, on board," Miko said, her eyes glued to the cats as they crept past, ignoring her and Echo as they closed the distance to their target. Sitting on the tarmac clutching his thigh, Pace failed to notice the situation had changed, that he was no longer the master.

Echo spun on her heels and followed Miko up the companionway and into the ship. She threw herself through the hatchway as a blood-curdling scream came from behind.

*One down,* she counted. *One to go.*

# Chapter Fourteen

ALEX KALLISTER GAZED UP to where the scaffolding vanished into the rock ceiling. Two separate cars ran up and down the shaft, one descending as the other ascended. Controlled from either top or bottom, they had little value as a way of escaping the mine. The minute he tried to use them, the guards above would know, and the second the gate opened at the surface, the occupants of the car would be welcomed with a blaze of weapons fire.

On the other side of the coin, the lifts would not help Pace's men either, for the same reason. Only the ramp remained. Over a thousand meters long, it doubled back on itself at the halfway point to emerge on the side of the original surface open cut, not far from the pithead.

Alex turned to take in the layout and contents of the vast chamber of the depot. Several dozen pieces of heavy machinery were parked there, including a massive bulldozer, loaders, and several ore trucks.

Over by the vehicles, his daughter Diana helped one of the more debilitated prisoners. Of all the problems swirling through his mind, she dominated his thoughts most of all. Her arrival with the rescue team had shocked him deeply. He had left her well away and safe, but now she was here, her continued chances of existence as grim as his, and of everyone in this chamber.

Walking across to a loader, he peered up at the cockpit. "Can we rustle up keys for these things?" He directed the question to no one in particular, but within minutes, a rebel ran up and emptied a box on the ground. Several men busied themselves sorting through the pile, locating and testing the key sets for each machine and vehicle.

Alex grinned to himself. The dozer's enormous blade, used to maintain the main thoroughfares in the vast mine system, was four meters wide and over two in height, and he intended to drive it at the head of a convoy. If he could get the monster to the surface without hitting the walls and collapsing the tunnel—he had never driven one before—it would act as a shield while the trucks, loaded with prisoners, made a break for the exit.

One of his men stepped up beside him. "Do you reckon it can work?"

"No idea. I don't think we have any other choice. Try to walk out of the entrance, and they'll cut us down. Stay here and we starve, or they find a way to kill us. Gas down the elevator shafts—something like that."

"I sent men to check the other back tunnel—both are collapsed, so we have no other way out. None we know about, anyway."

"Fine. The ramp it is. We take our chances up above, or die down here."

\* \* \*

Ben settled himself into the familiar embrace of the captain's chair. It felt good to be back in control, and now someone would pay for taking his command away from him.

151

Minutes earlier, he had snuck on board, leaving his medical officer and Echo at the foot of the gangway. Miko was an efficient medic, but was inclined to save lives, not take them. For this operation, he needed fighters, not saviors. Echo was more than adequate in any confrontation, but he wanted someone capable guarding his rear. Her bow was of limited value inside the cabin, and besides, six men had been enough to deal with two pirates.

The retaking of the destroyer took less than a minute. Occupied with preparing the spacecraft for flight, Pace's men failed to hear the new arrivals until it was too late. Ben and his men stormed the bridge deck, cutting down the pirates without hesitation.

Intent on securing his command, Ben did not notice what was going on outside, beneath the hull. Not until they dragged the bodies back to the service area did he realise what was happening. The women stood in the airlock bay, the hatch closed. When he opened it again to allow the ejection of the bodies, Ben spotted the bloodied remains of a corpse on the tarmac below.

Echo slumped against a wall bench. "Gordon Pace. His pet pussycats took a slight dislike to him."

The exterior cameras showed more men approaching from the hangar, only to drop in their tracks before they were anywhere near the ship. Ben sent a mental vote of thanks to the rebels remaining beyond the fence line.

Jerry Bayer slid into the pilot's seat. "There are ships everywhere above us," he said. "Not all from here, either."

"Take us up," Ben reaching for the intercom. "This is Fleet destroyer G4973, Ben Teague commanding, calling incoming vessels. Please identify yourself."

For a moment, he received no response, then, "G4973, this is Fleet Command Vessel C997. Baulk here. You sound pretty good for a dead man."

"Not quite dead, Captain. Just temporarily out of action. What is your status?"

"I am approaching the colony with two troop carriers. I intend to land on the airstrip. I have three destroyers pursuing several ships towards the outer system. What is your situation, Captain Teague?"

Ben considered his options. With troop ships about to arrive on the strip, it was safe to leave the mine to them. Each carried one hundred armed soldiers; they would deal with Pace's rabble army and free the prisoners in short order.

"I am lifting off now, and I am fully operational," he said. "I await your directions."

"A large freighter has just taken off and is heading around the planet. I have no spare ships to pursue it. Perhaps you can do me the favor?"

"Done," Ben responded. Without waiting for orders, Jerry lifted the ship and sent it thundering up through the atmosphere in pursuit of Marc Pace's vessel.

*   *   *

Beyond the fence, David waited as the cats finished their task and then stalked away. Their primary motivation had not been food, but revenge upon the human who bent them to his will for so long; once he was dead, they lost interest and moved off.

As soon as Echo and Miko entered the spacecraft, the hatch closed, re-opening minutes later to allow the bodies of two of Pace's henchmen to be ejected. David hesitated;

aware now that Diana must still be underground, he weighed up how best to help her.

There was no movement on the tarmac, and the corpses still possessed weapons. His team possessed only old projectile rifles, knives, and a crossbow, but meters away, lasers waited for the taking. Each of the two men ejected from the destroyer carried a pistol on his belt, and another lay on the ground beside the bloodied body of Gordon Pace.

The remaining guards stepped from the hangar door. Guns at the ready, they moved with caution, having seen the beasts attack their leader. Their current predicament was of more concern than the presence of any rebels. Nearby, several rifles were aimed and fired. The men dropped in their tracks, unaware of their real attackers.

"We need those guns," David whispered. "Then we head for the pithead, otherwise, our guys stay trapped in the mine."

"Teague can fix that with his gunship," Mattius said.

"I think he has something else in mind," David said, as the engines on Ben's destroyer wound up, drowning out all further conversation. At least half of the ships on the airstrip had taken off with the surviving members of the Pace family. David suspected Ben intended to go after them, leaving the ground battle to the approaching squadron Gordon Pace had spoken of minutes earlier. With a wave of his arm to draw the attention of the other rebels, David dropped from his tree perch and headed towards the fence.

He pushed through the gap in the wire and rushed across to the bodies on the tarmac. After retrieving the weapons, he and his companions moved away toward the mine.

*  *  *

Inside the depot, Alex stood by his daughter, watching as two of the men crept up the ramp. Their task was to test the water, to discover what waited at the top. Alex knew the pirates would be there, but he needed an idea of their strength. Another of his men stepped up beside them.

"We fixed the elevators," the newcomer reported. "Anyone trying to come down is in for one hell of a shock."

The elevator tracks had been booby-trapped with obstructive clamps, blocking the cage runners above the point where they exited the vertical shaft. Guards attempting to descend would be stuck until pulled back up again.

"Fine," Alex said. "Let's go." He and several other men followed the first two, maintaining a good degree of separation. Diana stayed behind, returning to where the prisoners crowded in a back corner of the main bay. Many of them were in appalling condition, the result of months, and sometimes years, of harsh treatment, overwork, and near starvation.

Alex moved slowly, his eyes focused ahead. When the leading rebels reached the switchback and vanished from view, he increased his pace, reaching the bend minutes later. As his men drew closer to the tunnel exit, they moved forward at a crouch, their weapons at the ready.

The upper ramp was dead straight and well lit. No lights shone outside, and with the ramp flooded with light, it would be easy for the guards to spot anyone ascending while themselves remaining hidden under the cover of darkness outside.

Because of the slope of the tunnel, the apron was invisible from some distance down. As they approached the critical point Alex's men slowed, moving to either side. With their backs against the walls, they inched forward, straining to see what lay outside.

Little was visible beyond the exit. A sheer wall constructed from the blades of giant excavators stretched in an arc, curving around to form a barrier to any attempted escape.

There was no sign of movement, and no sound other than the roar of spacecraft taking off from the nearby airstrip. One man, risking his life to advance to the exit, peered around the corner of the entrance and saw that the dozer wall ended clear of the cut face by several meters. He stepped back and returned to where Kallister stood waiting.

"There's a trap up there, Boss," the rebel said. "They let me go all the way up without shooting, so they're trying to pretend there's nobody up there. Machines are blocking the way out, mostly bulldozers. We can't go through them, but we might get out at the side. There's a gap there. I couldn't see any men, so the Gods know how many are there."

"Every man Pace has got," Alex spat. "They'll wait until we make a break and then hit us. Dozers, you say?"

"Yes, Boss."

"Right." He turned back down the tunnel. "Two can play that game."

Most machines in the mine, when not in actual use, remained parked in the depot. Among them were five huge ore trucks, the main users of the access ramp. The raw gold-bearing material dug from the earth went topside to the crushing plant in these vehicles, but now they sat unused to one side of the depot. As Alex returned below, a sixth truck rumbled into view along a thoroughfare. Found at the actual mine face, it was retrieved at his command.

At the rear of the bay, the massive caterpillar dozer roared to life. It was smaller than the ones on the apron above, but still massive, and the two-meter-high steel scoop would serve as the perfect shield.

"Get everyone into the backs of the trucks, and anything else you can find," Alex ordered as his men gathered around him. "Tell them to keep low and use the tray sides as protection. I'm going up first in the dozer, and the rest of you will follow me. As soon as you get out of the entrance, turn hard left and head out towards the gates. If they are closed, go straight through them. If they're blocked, go through the fences."

"What about you, boss?" someone asked. "That clunker of a dozer can't outrun shit."

"Don't worry about me. I'll follow on behind. Once we make it out, we divide and scatter. We'll meet at the Sandrine Gorge Bridge and head along the coast. Pace doesn't have enough men to chase us all."

"He won't need to leave guards here if we all run," a voice in the back of the group commented.

"Still won't be enough. Di, you are in the second truck."

Diana did not respond, tears trickling over her cheeks. It was obvious what her father intended to do, and that he might die. She would not let that happen. Determined to prevent it, she stepped up and whispered in his ear. "Got a minute, Dad?" she asked. "We found something interesting in a store room at the back."

\* \* \*

On the apron above, Barrett Harlow crouched in the shadow of his makeshift steel wall. Minutes earlier, he had watched a rebel creep up to the top of the ramp and survey the area, the machinery barrier, and the opening left at one end. With no light outside, they could not see the men hidden behind the massive blades of the dozers.

Out of service, the giant excavators had been parked in a vacant lot at the back of the main compound for over a decade. At Gordon Pace's insistence, Harlow kept them in operational order, for reasons he never understood. Now he thanked the gods for the foresight. The colossal steel blades formed an impenetrable barrier.

Soon or later, Kallister would have to come out, since the mines contained little in the way of food and water. With no choice but to turn left towards the only available exit, they were vulnerable to the little surprise he held in store.

Somewhere overhead, he heard a roar as another ship lifted from the airstrip and vanished into the night sky. The exodus concerned him. He did not doubt his ability to contain the rebels, but wondered what the Pace clan was doing and why so many people were boarding the ships.

On the way to the mine head, he recognized several members of the Pace clan coming down from the town. They appeared to be leaving en masse, but he assumed they would be back. There was no doubt the uprising would be over shortly, and an evacuation was an unnecessary waste of effort under the circumstances.

Movement at the shaft entrance caught his eye. The old road dozer from the tunnels trundled up the ramp and onto the apron. Close behind, a string of assorted mine machines emerged, turning to one side to form a line between the tunnel and the end of the barrier.

*What the f... are you doing, Kallister?*

158

The bulldozer trundled forward, its scoop raised to provide a shield. Harlow flicked his radio and ordered the exterior lights on; at once, the rebel strategy became obvious.

The enormous juggernaut rolled slowly on. The other machines stopped in a line towards the gap around the barricade end, the drivers sprinting back to the mine entrance. The rebels, Harlow realized, intended to create a wall of steel to shelter behind while making their break.

"Fire on the dozer," Harlow yelled. With the area now flooded with light, two figures were visible seated in the cab of the oncoming machine. The solid armor glass, barely visible behind the blade, might protect them from lasers, he thought, but not from what he intended. On a wave from his hand, half a dozen grenade launchers came to bear, and as many explosive missiles launched in a blaze of flaming exhaust.

The rumbling behemoth continued unperturbed as almost all the grenades hit the blade. The effect was negligible; the steel-encased engine, well shielded behind the blade, still running, the tracks undamaged. The blade itself was barely scratched. One missile hit the top of the cab, cracking but not shattering the armored glass.

"Damn it, re-load," Harlow screamed. The unstoppable machine ploughed closer, and as it rumbled to within a few meters distance, Harlow noticed something that sent a chill down his spine. Every square meter of the cab was packed with something he could not quite recognize. Stranger still, a fine wire trailed along the ground behind, all the way back to the tunnel entrance.

*What in the Gods' names ...?*

He never finished the thought. Before the second wave of grenades could be launched, the juggernaut hit the barrier and exploded with a force greater than any seen on the planet since the days of open-cut blasting.

Well down the ramp, safe behind the switchback, Alex Kallister lay flat behind a shield of machinery as the dozer erupted. Guessing his opponent's intention, he had prepared a small surprise of his own. The massive machine bulged with bale upon bale of high-explosive charges taken from the stores in the shafts. Rigged with detonators, three tonnes of plastic explosive ignited with a punch so powerful the apron vanished under a blanket of fire and smoke.

Despite their size, the excavators failed to withstand the sheer force, most of them pushed backwards several meters. The mine equipment had been the real diversion, intended not as the shelter Harlow assumed, but as a distraction while the bulldozer moved into position.

The damage to the machinery was minor compared to the effect on Harlow's men. Many died in an instant, despite the protection afforded by the blades of the steel barrier. Of the almost one hundred men on the barricade, only a handful remained in any condition to fight.

The second the charge triggered, Alex signaled for his people to move. As the first vehicle rolled past, he jumped on the runner. Further back, his daughter grinned at him from the next truck.

The entire plan had been hers. She was, he thought, cleverer than he had ever given her credit for. He had intended to drive the dozer himself as the primary distraction, at the possible expense of his own life, but Diana had decided otherwise. The explosives were her idea, as were the bodies of two dead mine guards in the cab.

Alex had bailed out before reaching the top of the ramp and run for the safety of the hairpin bend. The caterpillar tracks kept the bomb running true for sufficient time to reach the barrier.

The trucks roared from the tunnel entrance and made for the opening with no resistance from the guards. Harlow rolled to his knees and tried to lift himself. His skin burned, and he heard nothing—the force from the blast had deafened him. Across the apron, trucks rushed away towards the main gates. He had failed.

As they moved away, something else distracted him. High above, a sleek, silver spacecraft descended, the deafening roar little more than a muffled rumble to his damaged ears. The Fleet roundel showed on its hull—it was a Federation ship, he realized. *How in all the Hells did they find their way here?*

Something poked him behind one ear. He turned his head and stared into the muzzle of a laser rifle, held by a young man wearing a worn and dirty merchant navy uniform. The end of the barrel shook as its owner fought to keep his hands steady, but the fire in his eyes gave no doubt he would pull the trigger, given the slightest provocation.

All along the barrier, what remained of Harlow's stunned and injured men were being relieved of their weapons, threatened by a mottled assortment of men and women armed with everything from lasers to old rifles and machetes.

"G-give up?" the rebel stuttered, poking the rifle towards his face.

# Chapter Fifteen

BEN FOCUSED HIS ATTENTION on the main viewer. It was good to be back at the helm with his crew safe, especially Echo, who sat in a bulkhead seat behind him.

Many times in the past few months, he had considered the consequences of losing his first command through trickery, but now the future looked brighter. The destroyer was his again and appeared to be undamaged.

The comfortable grip of the command chair restored his confidence. He recalled the day he lost the ship; he could have done nothing differently. Despite complying with every fleet regulation and taking all normal precautions, he had not anticipated a sneak attack from a helpless and friendly human vessel in need of help. Refusal to provide aid to an injured man had consequences no less dire.

Today's events would bring to justice a pirate operation responsible for the loss of many spacecraft over the last year, the enslavement of hundreds of people, and the oppression of thousands more. He would also receive credit for the return of a renegade world to the Federation.

The outcome was not, he realized, the result of his actions—Echo and young David were to thank for much of that. The backtrack beacon was quick thinking on the young man's part.

The people of this world would also benefit. Wrenched from the fold not by choice or intent but by the wormhole closing through a quirk of nature, the planet had since been held under a virtual dictatorship by the Pace family.

With a Federation squadron now in the system, the settlement would soon be free to find its own future. The company that initially set up the mining colony was long gone, so with the re-establishment of the rule of law, the royalties from the mines would belong to the community for use in rebuilding.

A soft beeping sound warned Ben that his target was in range.

"This is Terran Fleet destroyer G4973 calling unidentified freighter heading outbound. We are in pursuit and are within firing distance. You will alter course and return to *Kerac*."

There was no response.

"Jerry, fire lasers in a bracket please. Don't hit them … too much."

A brilliant red streak leapt from the nose of the destroyer, grazing the hull of the fleeing craft so closely that it was almost accidental that the ship remained undamaged.

"Do you always work that way, Captain?" a deep, steady voice came over the console. "Shoot before we can respond?"

Echo jumped up to stand behind Ben's chair. "Marc. He must be in command."

"David said civilians boarded at the airstrip," Ben said. "I'm guessing some of the Pace family and its retainers are on board."

"Why would they run? They can't leave the system, can they? Not if the fleet controls the gateway."

"You might be surprised. The wormhole itself is tiny, but the gate is hundreds of square kilometers in area and difficult to police. With a war on, we can't spare a squadron to do the job. Pace intends to hide somewhere in the system's outer regions and wait for things to settle before making a break for the gate. Odds are they would get through without being caught."

"So they'll escape if we don't stop them?"

Ben smiled to himself. "Oh, not much chance of that." He turned his attention back to the intercom. "Good afternoon, Captain Pace. May I ask what your intentions are?"

"If you think I will surrender, you are much mistaken," the smooth, silky voice replied. "My brother will be here soon, and you can fight it out with him."

"Perhaps if you paid more attention, you would realize this is your brother's ship following you, or more correctly, mine that you stole. This is Captain Teague speaking." A self-satisfied smirk spread across Ben's face. "I am sorry to tell you this, but your thug of a big brother is dead, killed by his pets. Poetic, don't you think?" There was silence over the radio, but the pirate vessel did not deviate.

Movement caught Echo's eye, and she turned to see Miko, the medical officer, float on to the bridge and position herself behind Jerry's seat. The woman stared down at the console with a frozen expression, but remained silent.

"You will alter course now," Ben ordered, "or I will stop you by force." The freighter neither slowed nor changed trajectory, ploughing on towards the outer system.

"Ben," Echo interrupted. "He said he was fitting the Tolleani disabling device to all their ships. That ship might have one."

"If it does, our Captain Pace is not up to speed," Ben said. "He appears to have forgotten about it, but I have not. We *do* have one on this ship. Always wanted to try it," he said. "Hope the bastard works."

Without hesitation, he punched at the panel on his armrest. Seconds elapsed while the destroyer's computers synced with those of the fleeing ship, then a list of the Pace ship's systems scrolled up on the screen before Ben. A second's deliberation, and he punched the screen. The destroyer's computers took control of the enemy ship's circuits and shut down its drive systems.

"Enemy target immobilized."

"How come he hasn't stopped?" Echo asked.

"Inertia. He has no power to maneuver, though. The device works a real treat—first chance I've had to test it."

"So what happens now?"

"Without power, he keeps drifting out into space until we can catch him and board. To be honest, I'm not sure I want to bother."

Marc Pace's voice came over the speaker. "Clever, Captain. Let me guess … the weapon you and your little whore stole from the Tolleani?"

"Better a whore than a traitor and murderer," Echo spat.

"Ah, Echo, I half suspected you would be there. Such a shame. We were so good together, you and I."

Ben turned to look at his woman. "What's that supposed to mean?"

"Oh, didn't she tell you?' Pace's voice continued. "She and I know each other quite well. Had a wonderful time on the *Galicia* before we arrived here."

Echo's face flushed pink. "He's exaggerating. I'll explain later."

"Don't bother," Ben replied with a grin. "Not my business. I was dead, remember? Captain Pace, you are under arrest for acts of theft, piracy, slavery, and treason. No doubt we can add more, but for now, that should be enough to put you in a prison hulk for life."

"That is not going to happen," said the voice on the intercom. As he spoke, lasers flared out from the rear of the freighter and splashed across the defensive shields of the destroyer. The shields flared in response, but the warship continued undamaged.

Ben snorted in annoyance. "That was not very nice. Jerry, fire a warning. Punch a few holes in his drive system."

Before the second in command could respond, Miko leaned forward and stabbed her fingers at the firing console. A dazzling blue-green toroid of plasma erupted from the nose of the warship, twisting across the intervening space until it hit the engine module of the freighter. Enveloped in a ball of heat-energy it could not resist, the major portion of the module disintegrated, reduced to component atoms. As the disabled hulk spun off course, Miko turned and floated off the bridge.

Ben turned to watch her leave. "Remind me never to piss her off," he said.

"You going to report that?" Jerry asked.

"No. I would have done the same regardless, and the freighter is still ours. I…"

Without warning, the ruined freighter erupted in an expanding ball of radiant energy. The shields on Ben's destroyer, still fifty kilometers astern, flared from the impact of debris from the blast. For a long, drawn-out minute, silence reigned on the command deck.

"He blew himself up," Echo whispered. I can't believe he did that. He killed his entire family."

"No, I expect their reactor overloaded and blew. The sister and mother will likely be on separate ships, and we'll catch them."

"What if they don't give up?"

"I doubt it. Being a Fleet officer, Marc had more to lose."

"But he's dead."

Jerry Bayer sighed, pushing back from his console. "Just as well, I suppose."

"Why? What about justice?"

Ben turned in his seat and looked at her. "Funny thing about Fleet: there are never any cases of treason during wartime—none the public ever hears about, at least. It would damage morale. Pace will be listed as missing for now."

"His bravery medal—it was all a lie. He told me so."

"Yes. We can have the award withdrawn, but the official line will have him lost in action until the war ends. Traitors are bad for the Fleet image."

Echo returned to the rear of the bridge and strapped herself into her seat. *You win again, Pace*, she thought. *Pity it was for gold and power—nothing worthwhile.*

\* \* \*

Over the next few weeks, the Fleet squadron captured or destroyed most of the renegade ships. Intending to hide in the outer reaches of the system and await a chance to sneak through the gateway to freedom, most were tracked by the positive-ion trails every vessel left in its wake.

Echo stood in the companionway of Ben's ship and waved goodbye. At the foot of the steps, David and Diana stood hand in hand. David had chosen to stay, to help his newfound love and her father return the colony to a workable economic concern once more. Echo would not see her friends again for a long time, but she knew they would be good together, and she would come back to visit someday.

All the bandit ships were in custody or destroyed, and Mark and Gordon Pace were dead. Their sister, mother, and many other implicated members of the family and its entourage would pay for the crimes committed against the people of *Kerac*.

The time had come to leave, and with it a new dilemma for Echo. She had her man back again, but his presence created a massive conflict with the new life upon which she had embarked. The choice was a simple one—him, or a career in Fleet.

The long delay caused by the attack on the *Galicia* and Echo's subsequent sojourn on *Kerac 5* meant she had missed her scheduled induction to the academy, and at first, she assumed the solution was obvious. She would return to *Cymbel 3* and take up where she left off, as Ben's partner.

Deep inside, she was unsure that was what she wanted. As long as Ben was a serving officer, he would not limit her, the chance of his dying in action always present. Once this war was over, he would continue patrol duty until his commission ended or he retired, and she would be back where this all started, alone and bored in her little apartment.

Ben assured her General Molliner would sort out the mess and secure a place for her in the next academy intake, pointing out her recent adventure would increase her chances of being accepted a second time. Then, a year without him, and eventual assignment to a ship—but not his.

That was unlikely, and as a crewmember of another vessel, she would be subject to the same rules as him. If she joined Fleet and graduated, she might never see him again, and it might be the end of their relationship. She was not sure she could cope with that, considering all they had been through together.

Her mind was set on a different future, and she did not want to give that up either. Danger was exciting, and helping people like the settlers on this world made her feel worthwhile.

On the other hand, she now acknowledged that action and excitement gave her a thrill unlike any she had experienced before in her life.

Not far away, shuttles prepared to take the last group of survivors from the pirate hijackings to a passenger ship now orbiting above the planet. Among them was old Captain Henry. The effects of his stay in the mines showed in his deteriorated condition, but he was still as irascible as ever.

Echo has spoken with him earlier, at which time he expressed an intention to retire. He would accept the hefty pension owed him by the shipping line, find a companion to keep him warm in his old age, and a nice, safe world on which to spend the rest of his life.

Diana and David planned to marry in the not-too-distant future. Against all odds, Alex Kallister had taken a liking to the young man, who, despite his youth and inexperience, always seemed to do the right thing. By releasing the beacon, he had done more for the people of *Kerac* than all Alex's attempts to protect his people. David was a quick thinker and, given time, would make a good leader. Just as well, since Diana had become firmly attached to him and took no notice of her father's opinions.

True to his word, the rebel Karl had taken a team to pursue and destroy the cats, unwilling to let them roam free in the colony.

With one last look at the faces below, Echo stepped back and allowed a crewmember to close and lock the hatch. The destroyer's first destination would be a return to *Cymbel 3* for Ben to give a complete report on the events on *Kerac*. Echo would go with him, since the passenger transports would travel to a different world.

On the control deck, she unfolded the spare seat from the rear bulkhead and strapped herself in, ready for takeoff, her mind oblivious to the surrounding activity. It took several minutes before she realized every member of the ship's crew was packed onto the cramped bridge, those not normally stationed there standing in any available space. They all looked at her.

Ben rose from his seat and stepped aft, squatting in front of her so his eyes were level with hers.

"Kaska told me we have you to thank for all this. He says you insisted on raiding the mine to rescue us despite his reservations, and that you convinced the women to fight. And those crossbows were inspirational. We, all of us, owe you our lives."

"It wasn't just me…"

"We all owe you, and we wanted to say how grateful we are." Reaching out, he took her hand and kissed it. "You know, Captain Baulk tells me the first results of the disabling device are coming in. We sent re-fitted ships out with every squad we could, and not a single loss since. Once we fit our entire fleet, the conflict could be over in a few years."

"You hope." Echo doubted the idea.

"Yeah, well, if the Tolleani don't agree to peace talks, I expect command will find an unoccupied planet in enemy territory and give them a demonstration of their doomsday weapon, assuming we can make it work. That should do the trick."

"So…?"

"So we can spend more time together in the future, depending on your decision about the Academy."

Echo said nothing, wondering where this was going, fighting hard to choke back the tears bubbling up inside.

"It's a wonderful career," Ben continued, "and when we win the war, the job will be far less dangerous. Peacekeeping duties and the like. I can't expect you to turn down a second chance, can I? And I can't offer you that kind of excitement."

"What are you saying?"

"Fleet can give you so much more than I can, but it's your choice. If you want it then go for it, but I will always be here for you, as long as you want me."

Echo gasped for breath. A few months ago, her choice would have been easy, but now there were other options to consider. Ben had assured her that they would replace both her award medal and school certificate upon returning to *Cymbel 3*. She might continue her studies while he was on patrol, and perhaps be a doctor, a scientist … something useful.

She had Ben back again, and when the war was over, they could spend more time together. She needed someone to fill in the gaps left by all the things in her life ripped away by circumstance.

Despite everything, she also wanted to follow her new chosen path and attend the academy. For once, she had the chance to finish something she had started. She had already seen a great deal of excitement for this life, but now she knew that danger excited her and made her feel alive in a way nothing else did. Staying with Ben did not preclude joining Fleet, but at this stage, there was no guarantee they would give her another chance, despite his belief.

"So what do I do now?" she wondered out loud.

"That, my lovely girl," Ben said, "is up to you."

The End

Echo's adventures continue in *ENEMY ALLY*

# Author's Note

## DID YOU ENJOY 'DARK WORLD'?
## IF SO, YOU CAN MAKE A BIG DIFFERENCE.

Dear Reader:

Reviews are the most powerful tool I have when it comes to getting attention for my books, and help bring them to the attention of other readers. They also increase the chances of better review and promotion sites picking the book up, and increase a book's visibility on major book sites such as Amazon.

If you've enjoyed 'Solitude's End' and have five minutes to spare, I would be eternally grateful if you would leave a review (an honest one, and as short as you like) on the book's review page at your **favorite bookstore, or on Goodreads or BookBub.**

Thank you
Mike Waller

# Excerpt — ENEMY ALLY

## An Echo's Way Adventure

THE PALE GLOW FROM a single, giant moon filtered through the dense trees to the nearby animal path, giving just sufficient illumination to ease the otherwise total black of the night forest.

The lack of light did not concern Echo. With night-vision goggles, she could see the surrounding ground easily as she lay prone in the tangled undergrowth, cushioned by the vegetation that surrounded and concealed her.

Faint noises.

Muffled rustling reached her ears from the darkness, betraying the passage of small creatures as they scurried through the night on a never-ending quest for the next meal. Echo ignored them. Nothing here could bite through the resilient fabric of her sortie-suit, and besides, matters that were more important concerned her now.

She reached up and fine-tuned the goggles to bring the nearby bush track into sharp focus. Just ahead, a pale-green line marked the way through the ghostly vegetation. Any minute, her enemy would pass that way.

Seven kilometers apart, Echo's camp and her opponent's base were separated by tangled forests, choking undergrowth, and broad grasslands, the ideal arena for tonight's mission.

Only two passable routes existed between the two. The longer and slower alternative was a goat track around the rugged cliffs of the box-canyon walls. The nearby animal path was the easier way, following the bank of a stream that wound over the flat valley floor.

One thing was certain: the enemy commander would choose the easy route and attack by coming this way in force. He was in for a surprise.

Echo understood her opponent well. The mission had time constraints, and the cliff passage took longer. This business had to be settled before the first rise of this world's sun. He was as aware of that as was she.

He would not only come this way but also would move with stealth and deliberation despite the time limitations. A creature of habit, he rarely rushed anything. Tonight, his predictable behavior would be his undoing.

Echo and her companions had sprinted through the night to a point two-thirds of the distance between the camps before concealing themselves. The enemy commander and his men would, she hoped, pass by without detecting them hidden in the undergrowth. It was a play-off as to who would win this battle, and she chose to gamble, knowing her opponent would not.

Head turned to one side, she pressed her lips tightly together and willed her body to keep as still as possible. A meter away, a dark figure lay prone in the undergrowth. Only two of her team accompanied her—the best two. The others remained behind, well hidden and ready for any attack on her camp. A trap awaited there for the unwary, at what would appear to be a poorly defended site.

Located in a small clearing on the southern side of the box canyon, her center of operations comprised little more than a few dome-tents surrounding a pole on which flew the blue pennant of her command. Below it, concealed behind a barrier of piled field-gear, two soldiers crouched at the ready, back-to-back and each keeping a wary eye.

Those men would never be enough to resist an attack by a larger group, and therein lay the trap. They were the bait.

Echo's defense was well prepared. Her squad consisted of ten, including herself, her two sharpshooters, and the two guarding the flag. The remaining five were hidden in the trees surrounding her camp, positioned to be above and behind any encroaching force. The enemy leader's biggest failings were his predictability, his unwillingness to take risks, and his complete self-assurance that he was always right. He did things by the book or not at all. How he attained his rank puzzled Echo, but she suspected it was through birth and privilege rather than ability. He would try to surround his target, and that would be his undoing. Once there, he would find himself under attack from both front and rear.

Her breakneck sprint through the night placed her much closer to his camp than to hers. If she reached her goal first, this mission would be a total success. Once he passed, she would move on and arrive while he was still en route. The risk was worth taking, and she prayed he would not try the same thing. It paid to know your enemy.

As she waited in the darkness, she allowed her mind to drift. Not long ago, this was the last place she would have expected to find herself. Seven eventful years had passed since the day the Tolleani invaded her planet, *Corros,* and destroyed everything she held dear, including her family, friends, and the home in which she grew up.

She had joined the Fleet academy, intending to become a flight officer after six months of intensive instruction. In times of war things, happened quickly, and after basic training, she was waiting for assignment as a junior navigator when something unexpected changed her course.

Her commanding officer proposed an alternative option: to take a tour with a special task force formed for the highest-level infiltration and rescue. Every member of the division was a volunteer, many of them officers. It was a hard and dangerous assignment, but Echo's commander thought her ideally suited. Echo possessed greater skills in ground warfare than did the average raw recruit, and to her commander, a spell in Special Forces seemed appropriate.

The division was a part of Fleet, with squads in each operational task force. Most of her service time would still be spent in space, but she would have a chance to show her ground skills as well. She accepted the proposal without hesitation.

Echo returned her attention to the moment, to reassure herself that her companions were still in position and well hidden from the track. In the dim moonlight, and this dense undergrowth, it was difficult to spot anyone in a matt-black sortie suit. She lay still, listening to the sound of her breathing, waiting for the first warning of an approach.

Only Ben, now her life partner—if any relationship in wartime could be called that—balked at her decision to join this force. At first, he had opposed her choice, but he capitulated because of a promise that he would never stand in her way, no matter what path she chose. They had seen little of each other since, and she had no idea where their relationship stood. She dreaded how it would feel if he were no longer there for her.

As the moon slid behind the clouds, the forest turned darker and became almost silent. Only the soft chatter of the occasional nocturnal creature disturbed the otherwise absolute quiet.

Minutes after Echo and her team concealed themselves, the faint sound of footfalls reached their ears. Whispers grew to the gentle crunch of multiple feet moving through the night. Echo lay motionless, her night-vision goggles raised enough to see boots as they moved past her position.

Holding her breath, she counted off as they passed. There were six soldiers in the group, more than expected. The enemy squad, like her own, consisted of ten in total, so four remained at their camp—four men between her and her target.

For a moment longer, she waited as the footfalls faded. Her home team would have the advantage; seven against six was acceptable odds. For her, three against four was less so, but the situation could be worse. With a wave of her hand to her companions, she moved away, two shadowy, silent figures moving in behind.

The moon reappeared. Two kilometers remained to reach the enemy camp, and Echo picked up speed as the bush gave way to clearer grassland. In the distance, black shadows marked another patch of forest on the far side of which a rocky buttress, mottled a ghostly gray in the moonlight, stood out from the cliffs lining the canyon's northern boundary. Her objective sat below the outcrop, an old, crumbled mining depot now little more than a derelict, concrete ruin.

Two hundred meters from the target, Echo stopped and waited for her companions to gather around. Crouched in the dense undergrowth, she raised her head and focused her night-vision on the scene ahead.

The ruins sat hard against the buttress, the rock wall forming the rear of the old structure. At the front of the flat roof, a flagpole stretched up for three meters, carrying a red pennant. Around the bottom of the pole, sandbags formed a forward-facing barrier. Echo saw movement. At least one soldier crouched there, in a high position from which he or she could see any approaching threat.

A jumbled wall of stone blocks and timber cut across in front of the old building. The other guards would be there, ready to take down anyone who attempted a frontal attack. The barrier would be no hindrance to heavy weaponry, but was more than adequate against the light-laser rifles carried by Echo and her team.

The site was approachable from the front or sides, and the enemy defense appeared to cover the obvious options. Approach from the rear was impossible because of the sheer rock face, and the enemy commander assumed his opponent had no choice but to attack from the front. Echo was never so accepting. She studied the layout, searching for a flaw in his defense.

Off to one side, high grass spread along the foot of the cliffs to where a deep cleft split the rock. Enough to hide a climber, the crack extended up to the highest point on the buttress. Perfect. Echo waved her team closer.

"Katch," she said, addressing one of her companions in a low whisper. "Move around to the western side and up that big tree over there. Sarra, you do the same in those trees on the other side. Try to get a clear line of sight to the camp. You need to have a clean shot when the guards on the ground show themselves.

"I'm going for the buttress. I'll fire on them from above and force them to adjust their position. When they do, they'll show themselves, and you can take them out while I deal with the one under the flagpole. Go!"

As the others moved away to their appointed tasks, Echo crept through the trees on the eastern side seeking to reach the cliffs without being seen. Then she turned west and began the long crawl towards the buttress.

Voices drifted out from the base of the blockhouse, sounds of conversation and subdued laughter. The guards were not expecting an attack so early; it looked as if Echo's headlong rush across the valley might pay off.

Once through the tall grass, she eased into the rock crevice and began to climb. The gap was less than a meter across at the base and narrowed higher up—perfect for scaling. Ten minutes later, she reached the top and scrambled out to a narrow ledge. The position was exposed. Even with her head down, Echo ran a risk of being shot if spotted.

Luck stayed with her as the moon vanished once again, a solid shroud swallowing the stars as black rainclouds moved in. Bad weather was predicted, but so far, the rain had held off. She hoped it was the end of the moonlight for a while, or at least long enough to allow her to carry out her intended plan of attack.

With her rifle pushed ahead, she slithered along the ledge until she had a view of the roof of the old station and then braced, rising on her elbows sufficient to see her target.

Her original assessment had not quite been correct. Two guards sat behind the defensive barrier at the base of the flagpole, and not the one she had expected. One faced outward, peering into the night with her weapon propped on the barrier in front. Echo thanked the gods for the intermittent cloud cover, without which that guard might easily have spotted her team when it first emerged from the forest.

The second guard sat behind the first, legs splayed out and fiddling with his rifle. He faced towards Echo, head down and paying no attention to anything but the malfunctioning weapon. She determined to take him out last.

The possibility that the rifle was faulty might give her a few extra seconds.

*Staying alive 101*, she thought. *Make sure your gun is working* before *you need it to avoid being dead.*

Visible beyond the edge of the roof was the ground-level barrier, built around the ruined yard wall of the ancient outpost. The remaining two guards hid there, rifles at the ready, facing out and keeping low. They would be hard to hit from a frontal attack, their bodies well shielded by the makeshift fortifications.

Echo's team members were not attacking from the front. By now, they would be positioned as ordered and as high as possible. With the curve of the fortification wall, each enemy soldier was more exposed to attack from the sides.

Carefully, Echo aimed at the first of the rooftop guards. Sighting on the intricate harness of the body armor, she pressed the contact on her rifle. A bright, pencil-thin beam lashed out, hitting the enemy soldier squarely in the back. The webbing glowed green as a mild electric current made it stiffen, effectively neutralizing the wearer.

The second guard looked up and saw Echo, the malfunctioning weapon dropping from his hands as he lunged for the rifle of his downed companion and then struggled to rise to a firing position. Another bolt from Echo's laser hit his chest harness and released a web of current through his body armor. His loud cry alerted those below as he toppled forward, temporarily unable to move.

At ground level, the two remaining sentries turned towards the sound, raising their rifles as they searched for the source of the unexpected rear assault. They did not have time to retaliate. Laser fire from the trees on either side of the encampment cut them down as they rose from cover.

It took only seconds to dispatch all four guards; disabled by their armored suits, they lay motionless where they fell.

Echo climbed off the ledge and inched her way down the rock face to the roof. With barely a glance at the prone bodies, she scrambled to the flagpole, at the top of which flew the red pennant of the enemy, set in a metal socket.

Her rifle on her back, she wrapped herself around the pole and shimmied towards the top, reaching up until she could grasp the flag. With one heave, she lifted it free.

## End of Excerpt

## ABOUT THE AUTHOR

Mike Waller is a multi-award-winning writer of Science Fiction and Space Opera adventures, including the 'Echo's Way' stories and other stand-alone works. He currently lives in Queensland, Australia.

Mike's online home is at:

http://www.mikewallerauthor.com

You can connect with him on Facebook at:

http://www.facebook.com/AuthorMikeWaller/

You should email him at

mike.waller@mikewallerauthor.com

Mike answers every email received.

www.ingramcontent.com/pod-product-compliance
Lightning Source LLC
Chambersburg PA
CBHW030429120726
47903CB00003B/885